"All aboard!" the conductor called out.

"It's time, Alaina." Her mother hovered at her elbow like an anxious bird. "Your bag is aboard."

"Mother, *please.*" Her tears fell freely now, and she faced Jack again.

His eyes held a wet sheen that beckoned her own tears.

Charlotte retreated as the conductor shouted out another call.

"I've tried, Jack." She licked her lips and tasted salt. "I've tried, but I can't do this. I can't marry you."

His chest rose sharply, and he pulled her into his arms, where the scent of his damp shirt filled her nostrils and made her close her eyes against the desire to take back what she'd just said.

"Alaina, don't leave me," he whispered in her ear. "Don't leave me."

"People are more important than things, Jack."

"You are important to me."

"When you think of me."

"But I do, Alaina. All the time. I do it for—"

She couldn't bear to hear him say it yet again. She wrenched herself from his grasp just as the conductor gave his last warning and the train whistle rent the air.

S. DIONNE MOORE is a multi-published author who makes her home in Pennsylvania with her husband of twenty-one years and her daughter. You can visit her at www.sdionnemoore.com.

Promise of Tomorrow

S. Dionne Moore

Heartsong Presents

To my mother with love

A note from the Author:
I love to hear from my readers! You may correspond with me by writing:

S. Dionne Moore
Author Relations
PO Box 721
Uhrichsville, OH 44683

ISBN 978-1-60260-905-1

PROMISE OF TOMORROW

All scripture quotations are taken from the King James Version of the Bible.

All of the characters and events in this book are fictitious. Any resemblance to actual persons, living or dead, or to actual events is purely coincidental.

Our mission is to publish and distribute inspirational products offering exceptional value and biblical encouragement to the masses.

PRINTED IN THE U.S.A.

one

Jack Kelly stood cloaked in the shadow of a large tree. From this vantage point, his view of the woman he hoped to make his wife remained quite clear.

Alongside the lake, surrounded by veils of white dogwood blooms, the three Hensley children flocked around the skirts of Alaina Morrison's day dress. Her beatific smile beamed down on their heads. Alaina's close friend, Mary, off to the side of the group, laughed at the spectacle created as Alaina held the candy in her hand high above the shorter heads of their charges. Her voice carried to his hiding place. "Not until after supper. I promised your mother."

Jack drank in the scene. As one child, taller than the rest, made a jump for the candy, Alaina leaned into him with her free hand and offered a tickle to his ribs.

Mary calmed the growing frenzy of laughter with a clap of her hands. "We need to be heading home." Mary tapped the heads of two blond twins and an older girl and motioned. "Let's go before supper is declared too cold to eat."

"Do we have to go?" Little Lily Hensley whined to Alaina as she stood, grubby hands full of the pebbles prevalent at the lakeside retreat.

"We got here later than usual." She touched the tip of Lily's nose. "I'll allow five more minutes of playtime. How does that sound?"

Reinvigorated by the news, Lily clapped Alaina around the knees and the two went tumbling into a patch of spring green grass. Alaina sat up and started a tickle attack.

Jack crossed his arms, entranced by the vision before him. Alaina's yellow day dress did not flaunt the latest style. Plain but crisp, the material flattered her dark hair and eyes. The ease with which she laughed and smiled, accepted disappointments, and shared in fun swelled his heart, just as it had since he'd first talked to her at the store where her mother stitched clothing.

He'd seen her before that afternoon, but only at a distance. When she'd dropped three bolts of material at his feet and he'd helped to pick them up, her smile had made his heart pound and his palms sweat. He'd made the trip to the store across the river every spare moment for the past year and a half. At least until it had dawned on him that he loved her. But marriage meant he would need money.

He pushed the thought away as Alaina spread her arms wide. The smallest child of the prominent Hensley family toddled into her arms. She made a great show of allowing the little boy to help her to her feet, so much so that the two older children, Lily and Mark, pitched in to help.

With the light breeze from the lake at his back, and the promise of summer before him, Jack could no longer discount his feelings. For days he had reviewed his proposal, hesitant to say the words out loud, then unsure why he hesitated at all in asking Alaina to be his wife. But hesitate he did, and he hated himself at the end of every day he waited.

Today would be the day.

Alaina guided her small flock up the walkway toward Moorhead cottage, a large home that held little in common with its name. Built on the edge of Lake Conemaugh, the huge Queen Anne–style home, with its rounded end tower, was the summer retreat for any family rich enough to afford the rental price; a privilege Jack hoped to provide for Alaina someday. Of course, they would need to be members of the South Fork Fishing and Hunting Club first. But he held little doubt that as soon as he completed his invention, he would make that dream come true, too.

Jack turned his head and relished the bright sunshine that cast diamonds on the lake. Several boathouses squatted along the shore, waiting for the influx of summer club members to open their creaking doors and indulge in a little boating. Again, the sting of his inability to afford such luxuries stoked his determination.

Pushing his thoughts aside, Jack squinted toward the end of Lake Conemaugh, where a wide road crossed the breast of a tall dam. The view from the dam into the valley was breathtaking, one of Alaina's favorite spots. Satisfied with the location he had chosen, he inhaled to steady his nerves and returned his attention to the dark-haired beauty.

Alaina's steps brought her closer to him. Lily held her left hand, the three-year-old boy her right. Behind her trailed the twelve-year-old, trying to appear aloof from his siblings and "nanny."

Jack grinned. At twelve he would have done the same thing. He stepped out from beneath the tree and into the waning sunlight.

Thomas, the toddler, saw him first. He tugged Alaina's hand, pointing and drawing her attention to where Jack stood.

When she met his gaze, her expression softened, and she gave him a shy smile.

Jack laughed as Lily barreled into his legs. Her small face tilted back. "You bring me candy, Jack?"

"Lillian!" Alaina frowned. "Didn't I just say no more candy?"

"But Robert brings me candy." Lillian pouted.

Alaina's eyes flicked to his. She flinched, then glanced back to Lillian and held out her hand. "And you know how many times I've told Robert not to do that."

Jack tensed as he watched the flush creep up Alaina's neck. Robert. Again. The man's presence drove a thorn into Jack's side. They had worked together for the last year, a silent rivalry that extended from the workplace the moment Robert discovered his relationship with Alaina. He knew Alaina loved him, but sometimes Robert's persistence wore on him, and niggling doubts caused him to wonder if Alaina's gentle spirit somehow encouraged the man. His words came slowly. "Robert's daddy must be very rich to have so much candy."

Lily shook her head. "He doesn't have a daddy."

"Everyone has a daddy, silly," Alaina said.

"Big people don't." Lily's wide eyes beamed up at Jack.

Jack hesitated, the face of his rival flashed in his mind. He squatted down to look Lily in the eyes. "Robert is a big person, huh? How often does he come see you, Lils?" His voice directed the question at Lily, but his eyes flicked to Alaina.

She looked away.

"Lots." Lily tugged his hand. "Do you have a daddy?"

Jack felt the grip of that question as he stood. He shoved his hands into his pockets and forced a smile. "Miss Morrison is right. Everyone has a father."

Mark, the eldest Hensley boy, shot out from behind them and took the steps, two at a time, up to the porch. "We're gonna be late," he shouted from the top step.

Alaina placed Thomas's hand into Lily's and sent them up the steps. "I'll be along shortly. Make sure you wash your hands. Lily, you help Thomas."

The girl mumbled something and tugged her little brother along. On the third step, she paused and twisted around. "I don't have a father. I have a daddy."

"Come on," Mark yelled from the front door.

Jack cocked a brow. "Inquisitive, isn't she?"

"Very."

He waited for Alaina to look at him. She appeared weary, and he knew the subject of Robert, in her mind, was a closed one. "Robert's been pestering you again? Why didn't you tell me?"

"There's nothing to tell." She held his gaze. "He's been here twice, and I always send him away. He does it to antagonize you, you know."

Jack nodded. "I'll say something to him."

She raised a hand. "Don't."

Jack felt the first stab of irritation. "Why not?"

"Because I don't want to feed your animosity. You used to be great friends, remember?"

"Before you and I started seeing each other. A lot of things can change in a year." He saw the silent plea in her eyes and slid his hands into his pockets. If only he could afford a ring to slip onto her finger when he proposed. After he made good on his plans. "What I do, I do for us."

"Then let's put this subject aside for now and enjoy our time together." She lifted the front of her skirts and took the first step in the long flight to Hensley cottage, speaking over her shoulder. "I've got to get the children settled, and I'll be back."

The edge of his anger cooled as Jack watched her ascent.

She stopped halfway up and faced him. "You know, I've never heard you speak of your father before. Maybe—"

"Another subject to set aside." He cleared his throat to dispel the gruffness of his tone and forced a note of lightness into his voice. "Hurry back. I have a surprise for you."

"You do?"

"I do."

Her eyes sparkled. "I'll hurry." She made short work of the remaining steps and waggled her fingers at him before the door closed and blocked her from view.

Jack settled in for the wait. Mrs. Hensley's maid would take care of the children for the evening, but it was up to Alaina to get them settled for their supper before her duties were done. Ten minutes and she would be his.

His heart rate rose with anticipation. He rehearsed the speech he would make before the proposal. Should he kneel? Would she laugh? He patted his breast pocket to be sure he had a handkerchief in case she cried.

He straightened when the front door opened again and Alaina stepped onto the porch. At the top of the steps, she tilted her face toward the sun as if drinking in its energy. Jack's heart slammed against his ribs. He barreled up the steps.

She startled, a delicate hand at her throat. "You're crazy."

"Crazy in love."

She shook her head at him and stroked her hand down his cheek. "What am I going to do with you?"

Marry me. It was on the tip of his tongue to say the words, but he bit them back. He didn't want her memory of his proposal to be the front step of the Hensley rental.

In another burst of exuberance, Jack spanned her waist with his hands and lifted her down to the step even with him. She gasped at his action. When her feet were on solid ground again, he pulled her close.

She tilted her head back and jammed an elbow against his chest. "Really, Jack, I don't know what's gotten into you." Her gaze darted back to the house. "We need to be aware of who might be watching. You know the club doesn't like trespassers."

"You're not a trespasser. You work for them," Jack pointed out, but he gave her some room and satisfied himself with holding her hand.

"True. Neither of us are members, though, and that's what matters most to the owners."

"I'll be a member soon enough." He swelled his chest and winked. "When I get this promotion, I'll be well on my way to the presidency. Then we'll come up here as often as we please."

Jack tugged on her hand and allowed her to precede him down the stairs. As soon as he could, he twined his fingers with hers. He imagined himself a rich magnate and member of the exclusive club out strolling with his beautiful wife. His normal steps became a rolling strut.

She followed his pantomime and pretended to carry a parasol, head tilted at a lofty angle, her steps small but hurried.

At the end of the boardwalk, Jack could contain his laughter no longer.

Alaina's eyes sparkled as she, too, gave vent to the giggles stirred by their outrageous act. "If anyone should see us, they might think we're mocking."

"Oh, my lady, never us," he drawled. "We have lofty goals to attain such status ourselves."

Though her smile stayed, something died in Alaina's eyes. She bent to retrieve a handful of pebbles and tossed them into the mirrorlike surface at the edge of the lake.

Her silence sent gravel churning in his stomach. "Did I say something?" He touched her elbow. "Alaina?"

When she lifted her face, he could see the strain in her expression. "It's nothing, really. I think we've agreed to put aside unpleasant subjects. I don't want to spoil the evening."

Jack studied her profile a moment and then shrugged away his concern by changing the subject. "I brought a wagon from South Fork. I thought we might have our supper there this evening." His suggestion still did not rekindle the light in her eyes. Taking a deep breath, he braced himself and broached the subject he suspected caused her distress. "It's not you I don't trust, Alaina. It's Robert."

She gave him a wan smile. "Yes, but that doesn't end the strain between you two. Is this promotion really worth your friendship, Jack? Is money?"

How many times would he be forced to remind her? "I'm doing it for us."

He saw in her expression the moment she decided to let the argument alone. "Yes. I know."

Jack exhaled long and slow. Good. Still, shades of doubt niggled at his mind. The joy of his surprise seemed to have lessened considerably, and the weight of that made the moment flawed somehow.

As they neared Jack's rented wagon, she paused to fling more rocks into the lake. He took advantage of the opportunity to absorb her carefree attitude. Most young women wouldn't think about flinging dirty rocks, much less picking one up. Alaina had an easy way about her that soothed Jack, and her way with children never failed to delight him. He wanted children. Lots of children.

· With her.

He aided her ascent into the buggy and climbed in beside her, still unsure of what to do.

"Look!"

He followed her line of vision to see a heron rise from the lake. Another stood at the water's edge and craned its neck in their direction.

"Regal," he said and directed the wagon onto the road that crossed the dam. "We're coming up on the view."

The horse tugged the wagon along the road, harness jangling. Jack stopped the animal in the dead center of the road and went around to the other side of the wagon to help Alaina down.

Mottled green marked the stretching, yawning new leaves that peppered the trees in the narrow valley. Birds swooped and spun in dizzying patterns.

Jack refocused his attention on Alaina.

Her gentle smile lifted his spirits. Her eyes danced. "It's so beautiful."

For only a moment, he allowed the voice of caution to have sway. *I could ask her tomorrow night.*

As if sensing his stare, Alaina cast him a sidelong glance, brown eyes twinkling with mischief. "So is this my surprise?"

Jack softened and grasped her hand, his carefully rehearsed words scattered. But one thing he knew for certain. "I love you, Alaina Morrison."

ða

Alaina felt the grip of longing burn her throat as she gazed down into the valley toward Johnstown. She wanted to go home. On the other hand, if not for the Hensleys' early arrival, she would still be dodging her mother's not-so-subtle criticisms about women who settle for less than the best. Meaning Jack.

A breeze skimmed her brow and cooled her sun-warmed back. She closed her eyes to absorb the sights and sounds, the smells and feelings. Jack's surprise visit pleased her. She needed this—to be brought here by the man she loved and reminded of God's beauty.

If only the subject of Robert hadn't surfaced.

She became aware of Jack's stare and tilted her head in his direction. He reached to clasp her other hand. His declaration of love seemed so heartfelt. It pleased her to hear the words, as it had always pleased her, but as he tugged her toward him, the last emotion to settle in her heart and erode all others was one of confusion.

"You are beautiful," he whispered.

She cast about for something lighthearted to say and skimmed a finger over his upper lip. "I see that your mustache is coming right along. Very scoundrel-ish."

He raised his brows. "Scoundrel-ish? You said you liked mustaches. I think it makes me look dignified. And older."

"Yes, older." She shoved at him, laughing. "You look like you're fifty. If you had gray hair, I'd hand you a cane."

He laughed and waggled his brows. "I could marry Widow Sanford."

"She wouldn't have you."

He captured her free hand, his eyes suddenly serious and searching. "Would you?"

Alaina's breath halted. A breeze chilled her skin and ruffled his longish blond hair. In the depth of his eyes, she saw the sincerity of his question. She opened her mouth and gulped air, unable to form words.

"I think I'm going about this all wrong." He bent at the knee, never releasing her hands. His thumbs stroked along her knuckles, and he cleared his throat.

Her heart churned, and she glanced around in a fit of nerves. "Jack, people are looking."

"Does it matter?"

"I—" Alaina swallowed and faced him again as his hands tightened on hers.

Jack's eyes twinkled.

"No. You're right. Go ahead."

"Good, because this ground sure is hard."

"Roads usually are packed hard."

"I think I knelt on a rock."

"Then hurry."

"But what about the pretty speech I've rehearsed for the last two weeks?"

"Two weeks?" she gasped.

"Now, let's see. . . . Oh yes." Jack shifted his weight and cleared his throat. "Alaina, you've brought so much light into my life. I mean to make you proud of me. I need you. I want you by my side, to love me and be loved by me. Marry me, Alaina Morrison. Please."

Words wouldn't form on her lips, and she bit back the urge to giggle. What did a woman say when the man she loved asked her to marry him? "Yes" seemed so insufficient. Yet her heart beat so hard that she wasn't at all sure she could vocalize more than that small word. She pulled her hands away and touched Jack's elbows, urging him to his feet. She nodded, and the first tears started down her cheeks.

He produced a handkerchief, looking quite pleased with himself, and dabbed beneath her eyes.

"Yes, Jack. Yes." Not caring what or who was watching, she lunged into his arms. When she tried to pull back, his arms tightened.

His voice came out deep and rich. "Thank you." He released her and frowned a bit. "I wanted to give you a gold band but I—"

"I don't need one of those fancy rings, Jack."

"I'll buy you one as soon as I can set aside some money."

She stifled a sigh, not wanting to remind him that she didn't need expensive trifles to be happy. With great effort, she pushed away her frustration.

He raised her hand to his lips. "Always?"

"Always," she echoed.

After Jack had seen her to the door of Moorhead cottage and the warm glow of the evening had receded, Alaina lay for hours in the dark room, the sounds of Lily's breathing soft against her ear. She wiped away the tears from her cheeks. All the warnings of her mother, all the fears and doubts, came rushing back to her, until she could stand it no longer and slipped to her knees.

Lord, what have I done?

two

May 12, 1889

"He forgot you again?" Mary Hilton's eyebrows arched high.

Alaina turned toward the sullen lake waters and closed her eyes. She never should have mentioned it to her chattery friend. Blustery clouds and a chill wind promised an afternoon storm, but nothing compared to what Alaina felt in her heart. She bit her lip to hold back the tears as she gathered the food items into the basket. "He's a busy man. An important man, Mary. The company needs him."

Mary made a sound like an indignant snort. "What about you? What is he in love with, you or his job?"

Directly in front of the boardwalk from where they stood, an old rowboat had settled in muddy soil, no longer used for its original purpose but serving as a flowerpot. Spring geraniums, buds in abundance, petunias, and pansies all craned their necks toward the weak sunshine. Damp air rolled from the lake surface and spiraled around the two friends.

Alaina drew strength from God's beauty and waved her hand. "He is doing it for us."

"I think you should give Robert a chance." Mary hefted the picnic basket and called for her young charges. The children came running, jostling each other the whole way. She turned back to Alaina. "He is obviously interested in you. And he'll get the promotion before Jack will. He's been with the company longer."

Mary had her opinion and never shrank from expressing it, but sometimes Alaina wished her friend would bite down a little harder on her quick tongue.

"Robert would do anything for you, even move you away from grim little Johnstown." Mary motioned the children to go ahead of her. "Why, just yesterday he heard a visitor from the Midwest say Johnstown's sunrise began at ten o'clock and ended at two. How dreary is that? I definitely don't want to be stuck living here all my life."

Alaina had to agree with the visitor's description. Nestled between the mountains, Johnstown's sunny day did, indeed, begin later. Still, Alaina loved the place. The small city's bustle never failed to excite her. Even the constant drizzle of rain in the spring months did nothing to diminish her affection. To her, Johnstown held the best of both worlds. For in the moments when life became too stressful, she could always escape to the peaceful mountains. "That's just it." Alaina faced her friend. "I don't *want* to live anywhere else. I don't long for the big city like you do. Johnstown is my home."

Her friend looked skeptical. "But don't you get tired of it? And Jack is always forgetting you."

"He doesn't forget. He has to work on his plans when he has the chance. When he thinks he's on to something, he prefers not to break his concentration. You know how important this invention is to him. To us. And it's a long way up here from Johnstown."

"I'm happy for you, Lainey. Really." Mary touched her sleeve. "It's just that Jack is so unpredictable. I wonder what kind of husband he'll be."

Alaina felt the peace leak from her heart. She didn't want to answer. How many times had she asked herself that same question? Not wishing to take the conversation any further, she called to Thomas, Lily, and Mark.

"I'm sorry," Mary's voice whispered. "I want you to be happy, and if Jack makes you happy, then I'll say no more about it."

The Hensley children gathered around Alaina. "Go ahead and see your brother and sister home, Mark. I'll be right behind you."

Mark groaned. Lily, ever the little mother, grabbed Thomas's hand and practically pulled him over in her enthusiasm to get home.

"Slow down," Alaina admonished the little girl. "His legs aren't as long."

Mark herded his siblings up the boardwalk as Mary adjusted the picnic basket and shooed the twins ahead of her.

Alaina stole another glance at the sky. Dark clouds gathered on the horizon, and a rain-swept breeze filtered through her hair and caressed her cheek. Rain. Again. She inhaled the damp breeze and closed her eyes.

"You coming?"

Alaina's eyes popped open. She gave one more glance at the ever-darkening sky and hurried to catch up to Mary.

Her friend chuckled. "Woolgathering?"

"It looks like more rain is on the way."

Mary rolled her eyes. "As if we haven't had enough already." She snapped her fingers. "I almost forgot to tell you. The Garrens are only going to be here three more days."

"They're leaving early?"

Mary nodded. "Mrs. Garren said they wouldn't be needing me for as long as they had anticipated." She did a little bounce on the balls of her feet. "I'm really hoping she'll ask me to return with them to Philly as governess. Aren't the Hensleys leaving next week?"

"Yes. I found out yesterday morning." She skimmed the dull surface of the dark blue water. "I believe they're going to visit Mr. Carnegie's home in Cresson for a month. Then they'll return."

"Aren't you going with them to watch the children?"

She shook her head. "The Carnegies are arranging for a woman in Cresson to help with the children during the visit."

Mary's eyes glittered. She sighed. "I wish they would have asked me. I would have jumped at the chance to be inside that rich mansion with all those high society people."

Alaina frowned, disturbed by her friend's preoccupation

with all people rich.

Mary tilted her head and winked. "Does Jack know you'll be home next weekend?"

"I was going to surprise him." Last night, she almost said. She had envisioned his joy and the plans they would make to see the opera, go roller-skating, and take long walks in the evenings during her unexpected reprieve from the Hensleys.

"Well," Mary said, her voice a sympathetic whisper, "you've got a whole month to do as you please. Maybe Jack will finally invent whatever he's trying to invent, and you two can settle down and plan your wedding. If he gets the promotion, that'll be icing on the cake. Should satisfy your mother, too."

A dull throb began behind Alaina's eyes. The reality was, her mother was never satisfied.

As they turned onto the walkway leading to Moorhead cottage, Mary gave her a wan smile and squeezed her hand. "Gotta go, Lainey. I enjoyed the picnic. Like old times, right?"

three

Cambria Iron Works, Johnstown, Pennsylvania

Jack Kelly skidded into his boss's office. He pulled out a wadded handkerchief and mopped the sweat from his brow. Working in the constant and terrible heat of the blast furnace for twelve hours never failed to renew his determination to be the next shift manager.

Clarence Fulton didn't flinch at Jack's flurried entrance. His heavy brows shadowed his dark eyes, lending him a gaunt, haunted appearance.

"Good afternoon, Mr. Fulton." Jack inclined his head toward the man, stuffed his handkerchief back in his pocket, and held out his hand.

"Same to you, my boy." Fulton ignored Jack's proffered hand. "Sit down and tell me the latest on the progress of your plans."

Jack's finger roved inside his snug collar to release the sudden tightness against his neck. "I'm still working on the process, sir."

Clarence frowned and leaned forward, his chair belching a groan. "We've poured a lot of money into your research, Jack. I hope you are doing all you can to make sure the money is spent wisely. An invention such as you hope to spawn could revolutionize the steel industry."

Jack clasped his hands tight. His future depended on Clarence's patience. For long hours, Jack had studied the open-hearth process of turning iron ore into steel in hopes of inventing a method safer and quicker. He'd made pages and pages of notations whenever a new theory came to him. So far, none had worked. Now Clarence was obviously worried that his money was funneling into a chasm. Jack adjusted his collar again. He couldn't afford to do the research without Mr. Fulton's monetary backing. He forced himself to maintain an outward calm. "What are your fears, Mr. Fulton?"

"Fears? I wouldn't call them fears, Jack. Concerns, yes, but not fears. You come up with the solution to the slow process, one we can implement right here in Johnstown, and you'll be a very wealthy man." His eyes scraped down the length of Jack.

Jack witnessed Clarence's grimace of distaste at his disheveled appearance. He swallowed hard. "Yes, sir."

"I have another project for you." Clarence's palms smacked against the arms of his chair, and he pushed himself to a stand. "I want you to go up to that club and check on that dam. They've got a new civil engineer, I hear. I want to know what he's doing to insure the safety of the towns in line with that dam, Johnstown in particular."

"Mr. Morrell sent someone before and—"

"Daniel Morrell, God rest his soul, allowed those South Fork club snobs to put him off. I won't."

"They don't take kindly to people being there who don't belong," Jack said.

Clarence waved his hand in dismissal. "Not a problem. Your lady friend works up there for one of those fancy families, doesn't she? Go visit her."

Jack winced at the thought of facing Alaina after he ran out of time the previous night and was forced to choose between making the trek to South Fork or using his precious hours to work on his plans. He'd sent a telegram of regret to her, but unless she went to South Fork with the Hensleys, the chances Alaina got his message were slim.

Mr. Fulton crossed his arms and glared at a map of Johnstown on his wall. "The dam won't withstand all the water that club is filling it with for their fishing pleasure. If it crumbles"—he raised his hand, made a fist, and swiped it through the air—"Johnstown will be wiped out."

Jack nodded and leaned back. Every spring of the six years since he had moved to Johnstown, talk swirled among the townspeople about the South Fork Dam that held Lake Conemaugh. The dam hovered more than five hundred feet above Johnstown. Despite her love of the view the dam generated, Alaina, too, had expressed her fear of a breach many times. A break meant the water would sluice down the valley between the mountains and splash into Johnstown to form an enormous, deep, and deadly, puddle. Still, he had to be practical. Many men had examined the dam over the years. "Might I remind you, sir, that the last inspection indicated—"

"The last inspection was almost five years ago, boy." Clarence pinned him with a hard stare. "Between the April snow and all the rain this month, the rivers are already running high. We had bad floods in '85, '87, and last year. All we need is for the South Fork to bust open and we'll all be rowing down the river, whether we want to or not."

"It hasn't burst yet, sir."

"Yet." Fulton plopped down into his chair and tapped his fingers on the armrest. "Much more rain than this and history will be repeated. If we get doused, history, our history, just might end right here."

Jack cast about for a way to turn the conversation back to his research. He needed a little more time. Plans for a new theory for his invention were almost complete. He had a couple more tests to conduct on his working model. But working twelve-hour shifts made it difficult to find the time. And then there was Alaina.

When Mr. Fulton rose from his chair and regarded Jack in silence, he knew the meeting had come to an end. Jack nodded to his employer and scuttled toward the door.

"I like you, Jack. You're a hard worker. Keep working on those plans and report back to me in three days on the dam. Your diligence in this matter will position you well for that promotion, too." Clarence's lips curved in a semblance of a smile. "Hard work will take you far. Very far."

Elated at the implied promise in Clarence's words, Jack made his exit. He lengthened his stride and began to mentally run through his latest theory, checking and rechecking the process for errors.

"Licking the shoes of the bigwig again?"

He raised his head to see Robert Whitfield coming toward him down the hall. Robert's crude words piqued his ire. "Mr. Fulton knows I'm a dedicated worker. He calls on me when there's a job to be done."

"Or a promotion to be had?" Robert shook his head. "Nah. I've got this promotion in the bag, Jackie. Fulton's stringing you along to bleed what he can out of you, hoping you'll make him rich with your so-called invention." Robert's black hair, slicked to his head with sweat from the furnaces, lent his skin a pasty tint.

If not for the man's generous build, Jack would have laughed at his tough talk. He relaxed his fists, not realizing he had clenched them. Anything he said to Robert would filter back to Alaina through the ever-talkative Mary. He exhaled slowly and stepped around the man. "I've got to get back to work."

Jack's nemesis shrugged and continued down the hallway. "And I've got a meeting." He stopped in front of Clarence Fulton's door and sent Jack a sneering grin. "Can't keep Mr. Fulton waiting, can I?" He pitched his voice lower. "Wait until I'm your boss, Jackie. I'll have time for you and lots of it. Alaina won't give you a second glance once I get that promotion."

Something in Jack's chest unclenched at Robert's naive statement, and he found he could breathe again. "Really? Is that why she has agreed to become my wife?"

four

"I'll get it!" Five-year-old Lillian Hensley slipped on sock feet toward the front door. She stumbled when her foot caught on the edge of the carpet. Alaina stretched out her arm to stop the inevitable fall. No sooner had Alaina set Lily back on her feet when she shot toward the door. She struggled hard to open the thick oak plank, her tiny hands pushing against the frame to gain leverage. Finally, it cracked open.

"Why, if it's not little Lillian!"

Alaina heard the voice and saw Lily's huge grin. "You have candy?" The child reached up her arms as the man stepped into the foyer and into Alaina's line of vision. Robert Whitfield.

His dark eyes flared upon seeing her. "Good evening, Miss Alaina."

Lily's lip pooched. "I thought you came to see me."

Alaina grasped the doorknob for support and frowned at their guest. "He does come to see you, Lily. Doesn't he always say as much?"

Robert's eyes flicked over her. "I admit, there are others here who attract me as well."

Alaina gripped the doorknob tighter and hoped he would take her reluctance to close the door as a signal for him to leave. "Then you must have forgotten our last conversation, Mr. Whitfield."

"Mr. Whitfield, huh?" He set Lily on the floor and stooped to press a piece of candy into her palm. Three visits to Moorhead cottage and already Lily knew what to expect. Alaina only wished she knew Robert's intentions. Why wouldn't he stay away?

She worried the Hensleys might protest her visitor, though Mrs. Hensley never seemed to mind. In the absence of their housemaid, Alaina often greeted visitors at the door, with Lily as her ever-willing helper. Lily, scamp that she was, seemed to have a sixth sense when Robert was the person on the other side. Or maybe she smelled the candy offering he never failed to bring.

Robert's hand shot out and tugged the door from Alaina's grasp, swinging it closed.

Aware of Lily's wide-eyed stare watching her every move, Alaina placed a hand on the child's head and smiled. "Why don't you go play and let me talk to your friend."

"You won't send him away, will you?"

She met Robert's gaze. "Unless he has come to see your father or mother, yes, Mr. Whitfield will be leaving soon."

Robert leaned down and spoke in a loud whisper. "I'll bring four pieces of candy next time I come."

With obvious relief that her candy supply wouldn't dry up anytime soon, Lily nodded and skipped off down the wide hall.

Robert turned to Alaina, and she could see the hurt in his expression. "At least I have one fan."

Her words had come out more sharply than she had intended. She wanted to believe that Robert's intentions were good, just misdirected. "There are duties I need to tend to, Robert. Say what you have to say and let me get back to my work."

"Ah." He leaned in toward her and raised his brows. "We're back to first names. I like that."

She fumed at his sheer nerve. "What do you want?"

"Jack said you agreed to marry him."

"It's true."

"That's a shame. How can you be so devoted to a man who forgets you so often?"

Mary had obviously shared with Robert about Jack's latest broken promise. She turned toward the door and placed her hand on the doorknob. "I love him."

"Even when he doesn't show up to take you out? How

many times has he broken promises to you? Ten? Twenty? Seems a terrible foundation on which to build a marriage."

She felt his presence as he drew nearer, and she stiffened when he touched her elbow.

"Why not give me a chance?"

"Because—" Words died in her mind, and she struggled for a coherent reply. "Robert, please. Leave me alone."

"I'd treat you with the respect you deserve."

His presence disturbed her less than his words. First Mary, now him, expressing the exact fears she tortured herself with daily.

"I love you, Alaina." Robert's words slipped over her shoulder. "You'll be much happier with me."

She twisted the knob and eased the door open.

Robert, his words coming fast now, desperate, seemed to struggle for something to sway her.

"Besides, there's something about Jack you don't know."

"What would that be, Whitfield?"

Alaina gasped. Jack stood there, clearly having overheard Robert's last comment. His scowl smoldered, his blue eyes the color of an angry winter sky. She looked between the two men, afraid of the fire their sparks of anger might ignite.

Robert ignored Jack and slanted her a look. "I believe I'll leave that for you to figure out for yourself. I've quite apparently worn out my welcome. But please, Alaina, know that you have my deepest sympathy should you choose to marry him."

Her gaze flew to Jack's. She put a hand to his sleeve in silent supplication. Beneath her hand, his muscles relaxed.

Robert pressed his way forward. Jack moved aside and then followed the man's path down the steps. Alaina pulled Jack inside. "Your timing is perfect," she quipped to ease the tension.

"This time."

She saw the stress leave his expression in slow degrees as his eyes roved her face and hair.

"What did he have to say?"

"He was interested in finding out about our engagement." She hesitated, embarrassed to admit her own indiscretion. "Mary apparently told him that you didn't show up yesterday."

The recrimination she expected to see in his eyes didn't appear. Instead, Jack's face melted into a look of chagrin. He opened his arms wide. She nestled against him, his breath warm against her hair, the faint smell of lye soap drifting up from his clothes.

"I telegraphed to South Fork but knew you wouldn't get the message up here unless you happened to go down with the Hensleys for dinner or something. I'm sorry I didn't show up."

She closed her eyes. "Again."

He gave a solemn nod. "Yes. Again. Mr. Fulton called me to his office quite unexpectedly."

She brushed coal ash from the train off his sleeve. It smeared and clung. "You have ash all over you."

"Um," he mumbled against her hair.

Her mind jumped back and forth between her need to apologize and her pique at Jack's certainty that an apology was always going to be enough. She drew in a deep breath and swallowed, her words flowing on her exhale. "I should apologize as well. As much as I love Mary, she talks too much and tells Robert everything."

Jack drew away but held on to her hand. He glanced toward the stairs. "You're done for the evening?"

"Yes."

"Let's take a walk before I head back."

"What made you take the train?"

His eyes searched hers. "I knew I needed to get here to make up for yesterday." His finger traced the ridge of her knuckles. "I wanted to be here."

She felt her tension dissipate at his tender touch. "I have good news. The Hensleys are leaving next Wednesday and won't be back for a month."

"A month?"

"A whole month," she said. "I can start planning our wedding."

Jack blinked, the ghost of a frown pulled on his lips.

"Jack?"

"I'll have to test my new theory. I'm really hoping this time it will work. I could have enough money for us to buy a decent home."

"I don't mind living in Cambria City."

"*I* mind." He released her hand.

Alaina watched as he turned his back and crossed to the parlor doorway, hands stuffed in his trouser pockets. This core of determination she often felt in his character was the root cause for his driving himself, she was sure. But other than his oft-told story of being raised by a poor mother after his father left them, she never could glimpse the reason why he was so adamant they not live in Cambria City. He might have been raised poor, but so had she. At first she thought Jack's reasons were based on pride, but Jack never condescended to any of his friends who lived in the small city where employees of Cambria Iron Works rented homes. To remind him she didn't mind being poor would be wasted words. So she waited.

He stared into the parlor for several minutes before he returned to her and raised her left hand so their hands touched, palm to palm. His gaze commanded her attention. "I have to do this, Alaina. For me."

five

Johnstown, May 15, 1889

Alaina slipped into her mother's room, drawn by the snuffling snores and the promise of momentary peace her mother's slumber afforded. Charlotte Morrison slept on her back, hair bundled severely into a long braid. Smoothed by sleep, the etched frown lines could not lend her mother the perpetual sour look.

She debated whether to waken her mother and announce her presence. Tired from the day and the hustle of packing the Hensleys off, Alaina decided to wait. She had sent word last week that she would be home tonight. Apparently her mother had forgotten. She blinked back the burn of tears that threatened and released a sigh of pent-up frustration. She skimmed her mother's left hand and saw the slight, unnatural curl of the fingers grown sore from constant needlework.

Oh, Mother.

Alaina ran a gentle finger over her mother's hand and felt the roughness of skin chafed by the yards of material she measured out and sewed every day. "You work so hard," she whispered. Her mother's body flinched, and Alaina withdrew from the room on catlike feet and shut the door. She began to rehearse how to best tell her mother the news of her engagement.

Sleep eluded her. She wished Jack could have seen her home, but his shift at Cambria ended too late. He would stay later than the rest to work on his research and test his latest idea. Alaina raised her head and pounded the pillow. She shuddered and pulled the blanket tighter to her chin. Tears burned behind her eyelids.

29

Confusion and doubt returned to further torment her exhausted mind. And, beneath it all, the conviction that Robert would never treat their relationship so lightly. He had pursued her to the extreme, but she often wondered if he did so more to anger Jack than out of affection for her.

Robert's face floated through her memory, the way he had watched her as she'd begun to swing open the Hensleys' front door in an effort to hasten his exit. A knot tightened in her stomach. She pressed her hand there and swallowed against the ill feeling.

Something else, too. Something he'd said. . .

Alaina swept back her covers and swung her legs over the edge of the bed. Her mind churned to bring to full light what hid in the shadows.

There's something about Jack you don't know. . . .

That was it! But what had Robert meant?

Alaina walked to the window. Next door, a fine home made of brick stood bathed in the light of the full moon. Jack often flung his hand in the direction of that house and repeated his promise that he would buy her one someday. "When I've made my pile."

She shivered when a draft of cold air rushed through the room and forced her to take refuge under her blankets. Finally, sleep came.

When she next opened her eyes, her mother's frown greeted her.

ò

"He's got it out for you, Jack," Big Frank Mills huffed as he shoveled manganese into the ladle full of iron ore. "Watch yourself."

Jack sucked air into his tortured lungs and kept shoveling. Lathered in sweat, he gritted his teeth against the oppressive ache in muscles that begged him to stop. His reply never formed on his dry tongue, as the two men strained together to finish the job. Big Frank finally broke the pace. Jack didn't notice. His arms pumped hard.

"Easy. That's enough," Frank huffed. When Jack stopped, Big Frank passed him a cup of water. "Drink. Then drink again. You'll collapse in this heat."

"Look at you. You're not even sweating."

Frank guffawed and pulled off his thin-soled shoe. Water dripped out in a thin stream. "I reckon I'm all sweated out."

Jack leaned on his shovel and tipped the cup. He drained the contents and held it out for a refill. Frank tilted the bucket until Jack's cup overflowed onto the floor. "What did you mean earlier?"

Frank swiped his hand across his mouth and then ran his saturated handkerchief across his brow. "Our shift is almost over. You going to stay and experiment?"

"Not tonight." Jack let the shovel fall to the floor, relieved to see the greaser moving down the line. "Buddy's on his way to oil the machinery."

"We might as well head home then." Big Frank tilted the bucket and let the water run down his oversized head and shoulders. His teeth gleamed in the flashes of light from the open-hearth furnaces in front of them. "Next shift will have to fill their own bucket."

Jack drained his cup. "You're avoiding my question."

Big Frank lumbered away and gestured for Jack to follow. They emerged into the night air and allowed the breeze to cool their bodies.

"Who's got it out for me, Big Frank?"

Frank swerved his large head in Jack's direction. "You sure have a nose for trouble."

Jack hesitated. He chose his next words carefully. "You've probably heard that Alaina and I are engaged."

The Scot shook his head and delivered a gut-shaking slap on Jack's back. "Hadn't heard. Congratulations."

"Robert was the first to know."

"He's after you, boy," Frank said. "He sure had a hornet chasing him before you got here. Had a couple of the fellas askin' how it was you could be late and the boss didn't notice and did they want that in their new shift manager?"

"He's jealous."

Big Frank's hand sluiced water from his hair. "Old Mike told Robert to shut his trap and get out."

"I was only late by a couple of minutes. I woke up later than I wanted." A twinge of conscience pinched in Jack's gut. He should have guessed his tardiness would allow Robert the fodder he needed to make a case against him. "Mike knows Robert's trouble."

Frank's eyes were grave. "You need to remember something, though. Old Mike is almost done. He's as good as gone. If Robert can cause a big enough stink among the younger men, Fulton might not consider you for Mike's job just because the guys don't like you." He stroked a hand down his jaw. "I wouldn't put it past Robert and his cronies to cause an *accident* to put you out of the way for a while."

Accidents, Jack knew, occurred hourly, more toward the end of the twelve-hour shifts than the beginning. Carelessness ran rampant when the men grew weary. If Robert were to go so far as to do such a thing, he would have a lot of opportunities to pull it off.

Jack's eyes went to the ragged scar along Big Frank's forearm. A piece of slag had hit him and burned. The Scot had been lucky he had been a good distance away from the flying slag, or its velocity could have penetrated and killed him.

"That's part of the reason I want to make these ideas of mine work. We need a better way of doing this, Frank. Safer. The Bessemer is just the beginning." He clenched his fist. "I'll be on my guard for Robert's tricks."

Big Frank's hand clamped down on his shoulder. "And I'll be praying for you. Why don't you and Alaina come over for supper one evening? Missy and Sam would love to see you."

"I'll tell her," he said, though he knew he needed every spare moment to tweak his plans. Success was so close. It seemed to him the shape was the problem. The Bessemer's oval shape worked so well.

A flash of inspiration ran through his head as Jack raised his face to the evening sky. Mentally he reviewed the details of the new idea. Excitement coursed through him and renewed his strength. He would put the idea to the test as soon as his shift was over. Alaina wouldn't be home from South Fork. . . .

Jack ran a hand over his wet hair when he recalled the Hensleys' premature departure and Alaina's expected arrival in Johnstown last evening. His frustration grew. He needed to act on his new design as soon as possible, but Alaina would expect him, too.

Frank turned to head back inside and Jack followed. "You two going to tell her mama about your engagement?"

Jack's step faltered. "Why, yes. Sure. We'll let everyone know."

"Her mama's not going to be happy."

What energy Jack had felt moments before seemed to leak from him. "We're prepared for that."

Frank shouldered his cloth bag, and they left the building's stifling heat and constant noise. Big Frank chuckled. "You're not going to believe this, but Mrs. Morrison is a good woman deep down. A parent wants what they think is best for their child, even if they don't go about it the way they should. Mrs. Morrison's had her share of hurts, and sometimes you have to look beyond a person's hurt to see their heart. I'll be praying for you."

six

Clumps of oatmeal stuck in Alaina's throat with every bite. She finally gave up, shoved her bowl back, and pressed her palms together on the scarred wooden kitchen table, determined not to allow her mother's silence to continue. "Will you need my help today?"

Her mother appeared startled at her words. "No. I'm all caught up. I was expecting another order from Mrs. Stephens, so I worked ahead."

A new silence grew between them. Alaina worked her spoon around the small bowl.

"It's good to have you home again," Charlotte offered.

Alaina smiled at her mother's words, knowing that something unpleasant was coming. Her mother never offered loving words without tacking on a controversial issue.

"Your aunt wants to know when to expect you in Pittsburgh. I wrote back that the end of May is likely. It's a good time to look the college over."

Alaina forced herself not to release the pent-up sigh. Charlotte would take it as a show of anger. "I want to marry Jack, Mama."

Her mother's eyes moved over her face, examining.

Alaina placed her hands flat on the surface of the table. She braced herself for the flood of arguments her mother would rain down upon her. Jack was too young. *She* was too young. Jack was flighty and inconsistent. Jack's job wasn't good enough. They would struggle financially. And the one that all the others inevitably led up to—*she* needed to have a sound education before she married, so that if Jack, in his flighty inconsistency, left her alone, she would not live in poverty.

History repeated.

"I know how you feel." She paused, her eyes sweeping over her mother's graying hair. She softened her voice. "We want your blessing."

Charlotte Morrison's dark eyes glinted. "If you marry *him*, you won't have it."

Alaina's stomach clenched. In her mental list, she had forgotten that particular argument. The Robert-is-a-better-choice one. "I can't love a man I don't respect."

"Then why are you engaged to Jack?"

The gasp escaped before Alaina could steel herself. "How did you know?"

"So he did propose. Mary's mama said as much, but I didn't want to believe that you wouldn't tell me first. I knew something was up, though. I haven't seen Robert as much lately. Poor boy must be working hard to get that promotion."

She wanted to point out that Robert came to the apartment to see her, and being that she was in South Fork, it made sense that her mother wouldn't see him here. But stating such a fact would be foolish and mistook as irreverence. "You think Robert is so perfect, but you don't *know* him like I do, Mama."

Charlotte stood. Frown lines fanned out from her lips and creased her forehead. "You're right, I don't. But if Jack is as wonderful as you think he is, he won't mind waiting for you to get your education first. And you, being the wonderfully obedient daughter you should be, will listen to your mother."

Stung at the verbal assault, Alaina lowered her face and squeezed her eyes shut. "He's not like Daddy, Mother. Why do you have to compare my situation to yours? I know you work hard. I know we struggle. I've tried to help out as much as I can."

Her mother snatched up the bowls and set them on the edge of the dry sink. She squeezed behind Alaina to reach for her sewing apron and tied it on. "I don't have time for this right now. Mrs. Fortney will be in this morning, and I have three dresses that need some finishing touches." Without even so much as a good-bye, her mother slammed the door. Her steps clumped down the outside staircase that led to the back of the general store they lived above and where her mother worked.

Alaina surveyed the small apartment. Besides the dirty dishes, table, and dry sink, the room held only a tattered rag rug and an array of the colorful aprons her mother used to cover her clothes as she sewed. She noted the neat rows of pins stuck all along the skirt of the aprons. Every single one had scads of small, snipped threads clinging to the coarse material.

Two other rooms completed the apartment. Her mother's room was only as big as the grocer's pantry downstairs, and Alaina's room even smaller. But she loved the sunshine that streaked through her window on summer days. She often felt her room the better choice of the two because it had such a luxury. She smiled. And it had a tree. An old oak tree whose branches reached out to scrape the window on windy nights. Or held the weight of a young man who came calling in the night, though Jack hadn't made use of its thick limbs for many weeks.

Alaina crossed to the window and lifted the sash. A gusty breeze swept the room clean of the musty air always present in the wooden building during the rainy season. She inhaled deeply, braced her hands on the windowsill, and listened to the church's clock striking the hour. A layer of dark gray clouds promised more rain to come. Undaunted by the threat of a downpour, Alaina left the window open as she began to make beds and gather laundry.

With every passing year, it seemed Charlotte's expression became more dour, her attitude more bitter. Long ago, when the letters from her father still trickled in on rare occasion, Alaina learned not to ask questions of his whereabouts. And Charlotte had never made it a habit to mention him, her opinion boldly stated when she tossed the unread letter into the cookstove. But despite the veil of uncaring her mother hid behind, the letter stating her father had died had shattered something deep inside Charlotte.

Lord, what can I do? She heaved a sigh. It seemed the prayer had become a litany of late.

Alaina stopped at the open window and rested her hands on top of the broomstick. She rested her chin and closed her eyes. *Why am I so confused one moment and so sure of myself every time I look at Jack's smile or hear his laughter?* She pondered the half prayer and stilled herself to hear God's response.

The jangle of a harness outside the window snapped her to attention. Within seconds, the first drops of rain plinked against the window. Alaina slid the window shut, breathed on the glass, and wrote, *I love you, Jack.*

He had promised to come by after work so they could announce their engagement to her mother together, but the glow of the surprise was dimmed by Mary's tongue souring the secret and by Charlotte's staunch rejection of Jack. For whatever foolish reason, Alaina had thought maybe her mother's opinion of Jack would soften if the engagement became a reality.

Alaina lifted her mother's spare dress from a peg and folded it over her arm. She would try and talk to Charlotte one more time, during supper, before Jack arrived.

ஃ

Her mother got home later than usual. Splotches of rain dampened her hair and dotted her apron, but Alaina didn't miss her brief look of relief when she smelled supper cooking.

"Supper will be ready soon," Alaina offered unnecessarily.

Charlotte removed her apron and sagged into a kitchen chair. She flexed her fingers back and forth. "Rain always makes them worse."

"Maybe you should soak them tonight. I could run downstairs and buy some salts—"

"No need. I'll live."

And with that comment, Alaina knew her mother's petulance over their morning conversation had been remembered. She busied herself spooning up the beans and biscuits, wishing she had taken the extra time to purchase a chicken for frying.

She set the plate in front of her mother and took her seat opposite.

Her mother picked up her fork, stopped, met her gaze, and nodded. "Go ahead."

Alaina said a brief blessing that she suspected her mother forgot altogether when alone. She lifted her fork and tried to drum up a way to approach the subject of Jack without a wall going up between them. That was the trick. But Alaina could see no way to make that happen.

Best to be direct. It was easier. "I wondered if we could talk about Jack." Before her mother could finish chewing and give a caustic remark, she hurried on. "He's coming over tonight to ask permission to marry me, and I'd like for you to grant it." She bit the inside of her lip when she could think of nothing else to say.

Her mother set her fork down and stared at her. Alaina held her breath, waiting for the storm of her mother's emotions to break in with an angry flow of words. Instead, her mother blinked and averted her face. Charlotte's shoulders stooped, and her hands covered her face. Not until Alaina saw her shoulders heave and heard the first faint sniff did she realize what was happening.

Anger she could handle. Her mother's outbursts had become commonplace, but never before had she witnessed her mother's tears. She rounded the table and knelt beside Charlotte's chair. Glints of silver in her mother's hair reminded Alaina that she was the age her mother had been when she'd given birth to her. If only her father hadn't left them.

Her mother jerked to her feet. "I don't wish to be disturbed this evening. Jack Kelly is no longer welcome in this home, Alaina. Not tonight or ever again."

Alaina rocked back on her heels as her mother swept past, and the sound of the bedroom door lock clicking into place echoed deep in her spirit.

❦

Jack braced his feet apart and tilted his head way back to mark his target. His fingers jingled the pebbles in his trouser pocket. Alaina's window above the general store proved a challenge. He contemplated the nearby tree, but the lower branch he used to swing up had broken. He would have to think of something else.

He plucked a single pebble from his pocket and held it up between his thumb and forefinger to draw a bead on the window. A flick of his wrist and the pebble sailed through the air and tapped against the wood planks. Jack mentally adjusted his arc and launched another stone that hit the window with a gentle *tap*. Another followed. Then another. He waited in silence for any sign Alaina might have heard.

As he surrendered to the notion he would have to send a few more through the air, a dim light flickered and then flared to life. The window slid open, and Alaina gazed up at the sky, into the tree, then down at the ground. She gasped at the sight of him. "Jack!" She clamped a hand over her mouth, and her face disappeared from the window.

Jack grinned. He had surprised her.

She reappeared.

"Come down," he said in a loud whisper. The sight of her stole his breath. Her long hair tousled around her head. He could almost smell the warm scent of her skin.

Alaina didn't reply but again disappeared. The window whispered shut.

He waited at the base of the large maple, its branches studded with sprigs of small, spring leaves. He slicked a hand over his hair, still damp from his bath, and pursed his lips to whistle a tune before realizing the danger. Midnight was not the time to sing a cheery tune in the middle of the street. He satisfied himself with pacing in front of Heiser's store.

"What are you doing out here in the middle of the night?" Alaina's whisper cut across his thoughts, and he turned. She seemed to float toward him in the moonlight. Tendrils of hair brushed her cheeks and neck, a dark contrast against her creamy skin.

He took a step closer. Words stuck in his throat at the weight of her beauty. He caught her hands and lifted them to his chest. "I knew you would think I'd forgotten, so I wanted to surprise you."

"I knew you must be working on your plans again."

"It came to me tonight at the end of shift. I had to get it down on paper before I forgot. I think this time it's really going to work. You understand, don't you?"

Alaina blinked and stared at the ground.

Her hesitation made him nervous. "Mr. Fulton also asked me to look at the South Fork Dam. He's afraid it'll collapse under all this rain."

She tilted her head back, the slender column of her neck exposed in the pale moonlight. "More rain on the way, I'm afraid." Her voice sounded tremulous.

He grasped her hand and kissed the palm. "I wanted to be here to tell your mother the news, but Mr. Fulton gave me three days to report so I'll need to go tomorrow after shift. I'll come tomorrow evening as soon as I can and we'll tell her then."

Her expression went solemn, and when she opened her mouth to speak, he pressed a finger across her lips. "Wait, I have a surprise." Jack released her hand and plucked something from the ground at the base of the maple.

"A rose," she breathed.

"Mrs. Sanford's first. She'll skin me for cutting it, but I'll tell her it was for you and she'll get that dreamy look and I'll be off the hook."

In awe, he watched her bury her nose into the rose's blush petals. As she breathed in the sweet fragrance, an incredible vulnerability swept over him as he was reminded of his commitment to care for this woman. Slowly, he raised his hand to spiral a tendril of her hair around his finger. He released the coil. It stroked her cheek, and he mirrored the touch with his hand. Dark and luminous, her eyes caught at his heart.

He took a step closer and satisfied himself with brushing his lips against the cool skin of her brow. "When will you marry me?" His voice came out hoarse, and he cleared his throat.

Her gaze seemed fastened on his shirt. In the length of time it took her to answer, his mind tripped over what her hesitation might mean.

He drew away and held her by the shoulders. "Alaina?" Her head sunk lower. He felt the first indication of the depth of her distress in the vibration under his hands. The soft love in his heart bled away under the heat of his rising terror. "Lainie?"

"My mother knows we're engaged. She made a terrible scene this morning and then hardly talked to me after supper. She said—"

Her words choked off, and Jack's heart froze. He gave her a soft shake. "I'm here, Alaina. Tell me."

She raised her face, and he saw the despair in her expression. "She said you were no longer welcome in our home."

He pressed her close and willed himself to breathe as the next logical question begged to be asked. "How?"

Her shoulders quaked. "Mary. It's my fault, Jack."

His anger flared hot but cooled quickly. He couldn't expect Alaina not to share with her friend. She had to talk to someone, and Mary was the logical choice. He just wished the meddling girl would learn to keep a secret.

Alaina became silent in his arms. Her hair was silk under his stroking hand. "What do you want to do?"

"I don't want her to think I'm being obstinate. If I don't do as she asks, she'll accuse me of being an ungrateful daughter."

"You aren't. You know that, don't you?"

She nodded against his chest.

Recalling Big Frank's admonition, some great truth swelled in his heart. "Your mother is just hurt over your father leaving all those years ago. You can't blame her for that." He pulled back from her and tilted her chin upward. "You can't blame her for being afraid for you."

"She thinks you're like my father. Every time I told her you had forgotten a date. . .well, I finally stopped telling her because she would always say you were just like *him*."

"Meaning your daddy."

Her eyes glistened with unshed tears. "I wish I remembered him."

Jack pulled her close and buried his face in her hair. *And I wish I could forget mine.*

seven

May 17, 1889

Jack's report on the South Fork Dam took longer than he thought. The crinkled, yellow edges of the *Tribune*, dated 1881, reported that two of Johnstown's own men had inspected the dam and felt it stable enough to withstand the pressure of extra water. Those with doubts felt that even if it broke, the water had plenty of room to spread out before it hit Johnstown.

He laid the paper down on the rough tabletop in his small room and steepled his fingers under his chin. Exhaustion filtered through every muscle in his back.

The short, steep train ride up to South Fork after his long shift had given him time to study the terrain in detail and expanded on his own personal worry. The valley from Johnstown to South Fork was narrow, meaning the water would be like a huge, tall wall, barreling down the fourteen-foot drop to Johnstown like water in a sluice. Johnstown would be the dumping ground for every drop that came down the mountain. He ran the scenario of such a wall of water over in his mind, and every time he came up with the same answer—it would be devastating.

Jack rubbed at a spot above his eye where a dull throb had begun. He pulled over a stack of letters Fulton had given to him to examine. Correspondence between Morrell and B. F. Ruff, president of the club, read like the chronicles of two men used to having their own way, Morrell at least possessing the kinder tone of the two. Jack made a mental note of Morrell's suggestion that Ruff put in a drainage pipe and his offer to help finance the reconstruction of the dam. He searched through the stack for Ruff's response and didn't find one.

Another newspaper article in the stack reported on Daniel Morrell's acceptance into the South Fork Fishing and Hunting Club. An interesting fact that caused Jack to wonder if the membership had been a bribe on the part of the club. On the other hand, Daniel Morrell might have wanted to get an inside view of the club's doings. Could be that he was fully satisfied the club was doing all within its power to insure the safety of the dam and he simply wanted to be a part of such an organization. They would never know for sure, due to Morrell's death almost four years earlier.

Jack turned over his own ideas of the dam's issues and wrote his concerns on paper. To his eye, the dam buckled in the middle, the very place it needed to be strongest and highest. The drainage pipe was still a concern, and now with the heavy spring rains, if that earthen mound became soaked through. . .Jack wrote on paper his gut instinct—the dam remained unsafe.

He stretched, blew out the lantern, and uncurled from his chair. The dull throb in his head had become a steady ache. As he stripped off his clothes and lay his head down, his thoughts turned to Alaina. Longing swelled his heart. Her tears tore at him, and her mother's constant disapproval of him chipped away at his patience.

He flipped onto his back and lay with his arm across his eyes. Charlotte Morrison had no way of understanding Jack's drive. He sometimes wondered if Alaina understood or just endured. Sleep didn't fold him into its velvety arms as he'd hoped. Drafts floated in from the cracks in the walls and made him shiver. He pulled the blanket tighter around his chin and opened his eyes to the dark, hollow *ping* of rain against the roof.

With a grunt, he swept back the covers, crossed to the old kitchen cabinet hung on one wall, and retrieved a tin can. Even in the dark, he could see the water stain on the wood floor. His toes curled at the cold wood as he set the can beneath the spot where the leak always occurred. He squinted up to where the dull whitewashed ceiling sported a ragged gold ring. The first drop of water hit him on the forehead. Jack moved aside and tugged the can closer to the spot where he had been standing.

He stretched and scratched his chest. The clouds let loose with a tirade, and he waited for the inevitable. A sloppy *ping* let him know the can still lay out of line with the leak. He groaned and gave in, lit the lantern, and brought it back to the dark splotch of water, centering the can directly over the spot.

His landlady, Widow Sanford, had just had a bathroom installed in her home, along with a phone and steam heat, but the small shack Jack rented remained without those amenities. His relief at being left out of the so-called *improvements* was great. The last thing he needed was a rent hike.

He eyed the report on the table and allowed himself to dream about the benefits getting the promotion would give him. He had allowed Alaina to see the outside of his place only once and vowed then and there that he would not marry her unless he could provide better than the one-room shack.

The rhythmic *ping* of the water stripped him of his exhaustion. He went down on his knees beside his narrow cot and pulled out a box. Its top, carved with flowers and hearts, sketched in his mind a vision of his mother's long fingers tracing the same design, a sad smile on her face. He removed the lid and plunged his hand into the box to lift out the Bible. *Her* Bible, now his.

At the table he pulled the lantern close and opened the fine-tooled leather cover. Little notes in the margins, as familiar to him as the scar on the back of his hand, made him feel closer to his mother and, in turn, he felt closer to God. He turned to his favorite verse and read it, his mind automatically taking on his mother's voice as he repeated the words to himself.

"Thou wilt shew me the path of life: in thy presence is fulness of joy; at thy right hand there are pleasures for evermore."

Psalm 16:11. How many times had he heard his mother quote the scripture to him in his years growing up, even in those gray days after his father's death?

He squeezed his eyes shut, hands clenched tight. He saw Alaina's longing eyes as she expressed her desire to remember her father. Heard the flat sound of his mother's voice after that terrible night when she sat him on her knee and told him the news. Only later did he understand the shame that she had endured when the truth was made known.

Jack swallowed hard. He shut the Bible and noticed an edge of paper sticking out. Thinking to uncrease a bent corner, he traced the place with his finger and discovered a folded paper behind a loose cover flap. Jack tugged at the corner. It caught where the glued edge of the cover flap held it in place. With his finger, he pulled the flap away and tugged out the folded pages. He recognized the handwriting immediately as that of his father. He scanned the contents, realizing his mother must have kept the letter for a very good reason.

Dear Olivia,

You don't deserve this. Maybe your mother was right all along, you should have married Frederick Thomas. I don't know. I do know that you will be better off without me, as will Jack. I haven't touched a drop in over a month, just as I promised you, but another type of failure greeted me this afternoon while you were out—our bank failed. We've lost everything. It's too much for me. You're strong, Livey, much stronger than I. You'll survive and make a better home for Jack alone than you ever would with me in the picture.

I do love you. Please believe me, and when the time is right, tell Jack I love him, too.

Yours,
Don

Jack let the letter flutter from his hands to the floor. He leaned forward as if punched in the gut and pressed his thumbs against his eyes. Flashes from the past sliced through him, the last one from the day he watched his mother lowered into the ground. If not for his remembrance of her favorite verse, he might have been overwhelmed by his grief. Jack sucked in a deep breath and held it.

God, give me strength to forget. To forgive.

He released his breath and felt the tendrils of exhaustion weaving through his body.

eight

May 18, 1889

Alaina woke from a deep sleep to the touch of her mother's hand on her arm.

"I thought I'd better wake you before I left," her mother said.

She scooted up in bed, fully expecting her mother to turn and leave, surprised when she stayed.

Charlotte stood still, her eyes on the far wall.

Alarmed, Alaina scooted up in bed and noted her mother's puffy, red eyes and pale complexion.

"Mama, are you ill?"

Charlotte's gaze snapped to hers. "I'll be fine." But she still didn't move.

Alaina grasped her mother's arms. "Mother, please, what's the matter?"

Charlotte's eyes filled with tears. Her mother pressed a hand to Alaina's cheek, then spun and left the room.

Alaina skittered on the edge of concern all morning, not at all sure what to make of her mother's unusual behavior. After she dressed, she decided a quick visit to the store after chores might help alleviate her fears. If her mother was truly ill, she needed to know.

Laundry took all day, and it wasn't until early evening that she got the chance to escape to the store. If Jack kept his promise, he would be here this evening. If only she could get her mother to talk to her first.

Through the back door of the store, Alaina could see Charlotte sitting in the corner, stitching on a long gown of tweed brown and gold. Surrounded by needles, pins, and spools of Clark's O.N.T., her mother appeared relaxed and serene, though her eyes still showed tinges of puffiness.

"Miss Morrison."

Alaina's attention flew to the young man coming toward her. Charlotte Morrison raised her head. Young Victor Heiser, the storekeeper's son, grinned at her with a mixture of shyness and longing.

"Good day to you, Victor. How are you?"

He seemed abashed that she answered him and lowered his head. "I'm doing well."

"And is Miss Powers doing well with the Sunday school?"

He peeked at her. "Yes, ma'am. Though you were the best teacher."

Alaina smiled her gratitude. "How kind of you. Give Miss Powers a chance, and I'm sure everyone will love her as much."

"I suppose." Victor's ears reddened and he shrugged. "Your mother asked me if I still remembered my scripture verses. I do. I repeated them all for her. All forty-two."

Alaina felt the edge of surprise that her mother would inquire. In the six months Alaina taught Sunday school, she had endeavored to commit two verses a week to memory and challenged her pupils to do the same. Friday and Saturday nights during the fall and winter, she had repeated them aloud as she went about her chores. Her mother had never shown the least interest. "You are to be commended, Victor. I don't know that I could do such a thing without first brushing up a bit."

"Oh, you could, Miss Alaina. I'm sure of it!"

She laughed at his enthusiasm. "Maybe I should pop into your class this Sunday. We could have a contest."

Mathilde Heiser, Victor's mother, appeared from the front of the store, her expression harried. "Victor, stop dawdling. Your father needs you." Mathilde gestured to the boy and then rolled her eyes over at Alaina. "How that boy does go on about you. I think you've stolen his heart and most of his head. I keep reminding him that he's no competition to Jack."

Alaina tilted her head and laughed. "I'm sure Jack won't feel threatened, Mrs. Heiser. How is your husband doing?"

"Very well. Your mother's skill has really been a draw for the womenfolk. She is very good."

Alaina smiled over at her mother. "Yes, she is."

Charlotte held up the dress she had been working on and shook it out, but Alaina saw the trace of a pleased smile on her lips. "You've both been very kind to me, Mrs. Heiser. Mr. Springer never seemed to appreciate a woman's need for a fine gown." She paused, her eyes lifting to Alaina. "I think it's about time for my daughter to have some new gowns, too. I wouldn't want the ladies to see the daughter of their seamstress in anything less than the best."

Victor rushed over to his mother and tugged on her sleeve. "Father needs us both."

Mrs. Heiser lifted her hand. "Whatever your mother does for you will be lovely."

Unconsciously, Alaina fingered the material of her blue dress. It used to be her best, but after months of wear, it had lost the luster of newness. She wanted to tell her mother not to worry about making her a new gown, but something about the offer stopped her. How long had it been since her mother last made such an offer? Alaina usually made her own gowns during the winter months. Her mother knew that. Something about Charlotte's offer seemed gentle and kind. Different.

Charlotte stuck a pin in her mouth and nodded. "What brought you down here?"

"I wanted to check on you."

The pin in her mother's mouth seemed to tremble, and Alaina thought she detected a sheen of tears in her eyes.

Her conscience pricked, and she whispered the next words. "I'm supposed to meet Jack this evening." Alaina expected to feel the singe of her mother's anger at the mention of Jack.

Instead, Charlotte merely sat down and reorganized the yards of material. "On your way out, tell Victor to come back when he gets the chance. I want to hear him recite those verses again."

Alaina pleaded with her eyes. "Jack will want to say hello."

Her mother's mouth drooped. "Tell him hello for me." Charlotte returned her attention to the material, her needle sliding in and out in impossibly small stitches.

Alaina headed to the front of the store. She stopped in the middle of the room and took in the bright display of candy and soap powder, medicines, and washboards. Unshed tears made everything a blur. She had so wanted to hear her mother acquiesce and welcome the opportunity of seeing Jack.

A hand appeared in front of her face, with a licorice whip dangling from long, calloused fingers. Her heart leaped and almost turned into the embrace of Jack's arms, but conscious of where they were, she took a step back and plucked the licorice from his hand.

"My, my, greedy, aren't we?"

"You tempt me with my favorite candy and you don't expect me to take the bait?"

Jack's expression held mischief. "I wish you were that excited to see me."

Alaina returned his smile. "Don't be silly."

He twined his fingers through hers and pulled her close enough to whisper in her ear. "One piece for you. I thought I'd make a peace offering with the rest."

"Jack." She shook her head and kept her voice low so other patrons wouldn't hear. "Mama told me to tell you hello. I don't think it's a good idea for us to push too hard right now." Though she loved him the more for wanting to try and make peace.

Jack glanced toward the back of the store and then at the bag of licorice in his free hand. He handed it over to her. "Then I'll surrender them to you for delivery. But you have to promise not to eat them all on your way back."

Alaina accepted the bag and gave him a rueful grin. "I'll try not to."

"Are you hungry?"

She held up the bag. "I won't be."

Jack touched the tip of her nose. "Let's go before I storm the back room and demand to marry you on the spot, with or without her blessing."

The lightness being in Jack's presence had brought faded as she retraced her steps back to her mother's corner of the store. Charlotte didn't look up from her sewing.

"Mama?" The bag crinkled in Alaina's hand as she slipped it onto the low table by her mother's stool.

Charlotte glanced at the parcel. "What's this?"

Her throat thickened and she swallowed. "Jack's peace offering." Before she broke into tears, she hurried back to the front of the store. With one glance, Jack must have understood her need, for he offered his arm and led her to the entrance, giving Victor Heiser, his eyes wide upon them, a slap on the back. He whispered something in the young man's ear, then turned and winked at Alaina.

Once outside, she demanded to know what he'd said to the boy.

"I told him the truth. You're too old for him." He leaned in so close she could feel his breath against her face. "Unless, of course, you prefer younger men."

The way he said it, his closeness, it made her heart beat madly. "No, there's only one for me."

His playful expression became serious. His gaze swept her face and caused her stomach to twist. Beneath the luminescent light in his blue eyes, heat rose in her cheeks.

"Well, then"—he took a deliberate step back and returned her hand to his arm—"if you won't marry me tonight, then we could go for a walk or roller-skating."

She laughed but sobered at the thought of her mother's scowl of disapproval upon learning they had married without her knowledge or blessing. Still. . . "Wouldn't it be wonderful to get married and—"

"Until we reached my place and I carried you over the

threshold." He gazed at the darkening sky of lead gray. "We could take turns emptying the mug of water from my leaky roof." The smile he sent her didn't reach his eyes. "Not what I want for you. For us."

"Then let's walk around and see the sights. We could go to the park and walk until dark."

Jack winced. "I can't stay too long. I need to finish my report to Mr. Fulton." He placed his hand over hers, where it lay nestled against his arm. "I also need to spend some time this evening working on my plans since church is tomorrow. I think I'm close, Alaina."

He must have sensed her disappointment because he kept talking, giving assurances, reminding her he did it for them, but she scarcely heard him. All the doubts tumbled around in her head and welled in her chest. His invention always seemed first priority, and she couldn't quite shake off the sincerity of her mother's many warnings against Jack.

"He is always chasing after his dream of money. Marry a man who will put you first."

And then there was the one her mother never directly spoke but Alaina felt in every line of sadness on her mother's face.

Your father chased after the dream of money and never returned.

She knew Jack wanted to earn a good living, but how far would he go to do that? Was his need driven by something in his past? Maybe his parents were rich and he had been disinherited.

Alaina slipped a glance over at Jack as he talked. They were engaged. Surely he could tell her about his mother and father. He knew all about hers. She had a right to know. Maybe it would help her understand him better.

She waited for a lull in his words. "Jack, tell me about your parents."

"My parents?"

The sudden shift in topics had taken him off guard. Something like panic seeped into his eyes.

"Yes. You always avoid the subject. I want to know about

them. Shouldn't I meet them before we marry? Don't you want to include them in our plans?"

Jack's face set like chiseled stone. She felt the wall of his anger rise with every second, brick by angry brick. "I'm an adult. I don't need their permission."

"Surely your mother would—"

He released her abruptly, his gaze full of pain. "She's dead, Alaina. My mother is dead. She won't care about a thing."

"What? How did it happen? I mean, when?"

A muscle jumped in his jaw. "A long time ago. Before I moved here."

"What about your father?"

His gaze went white-hot. He turned away, fists clenched at his sides. "It's a topic for another time."

She touched his arm and felt the taut bunch of his muscles. "Please, Jack."

He bowed his head and knotted fists rubbed his eyes.

Alaina felt his pain without understanding the reason for it. Shame washed over her at her insistence. "I'm sorry." She ran her hand down his upper arm to his wrist and then lifted his hand to gently uncurl his fingers, all the while silently begging him to look at her. *Please, Lord, take this hurt away.* She wanted so much to erase the entire conversation.

On another level, his reaction to the simple question chilled her. What did it mean? What was in his past that proved so painful it rendered him speechless?

Finally, she felt the tension leave him.

He squeezed his eyes shut and regarded her with a look of profound exhaustion, as if he had fought many demons in the last few minutes. "I've got to go," his voice scraped out.

"I understand."

"I'll walk you back."

"No." She forced a smile. "I'll be fine."

"Alaina. . ." He paused. "I need some time. It's not a topic I—"

"Then I'll wait."

nine

May 19, 1889

Alaina started upon seeing her mother, dressed and ready for Sunday morning services. She tried to recall the last service her mother had attended and settled on Easter, two years ago, when her aunt had come over from Pittsburgh for a short visit.

"You're dressed," she stated the obvious, then laughed.

The comment pulled a smile from her mother as she smoothed a strand of hair back from her face. "It's time, don't you think?" Her mother gathered the material of her best dress in one hand and frowned at the brown plaid. "I need to start on new dresses for both of us. This material is so thin at the elbows."

Her mother continued to fuss over the dress while Alaina tried to make sense of her question. What did she mean by, "It's time?" Time for what? Time to go? But no, it couldn't be. Jack wouldn't arrive to fetch her for another twenty minutes.

"Alaina?" her mother asked. "Would you fetch my Bible?"

She did as bid, expecting the Book to be collecting dust on the small table her mother used to hold a lamp. To her surprise and satisfaction, she saw that the Bible lay open on the table and rejoiced at the implication. It had been such a long time since Father had left. Perhaps her mother would return to the faith she had once held so dear.

She searched for a way to bring up the topic of her mother's sudden Bible reading and churchgoing when Jack arrived. Upon seeing him, her mother's frown deepened. Alaina feared she might say something harsh, but Charlotte nodded in response to Jack's greeting and allowed him to help her into the hackney with a small smile bestowed on him as his reward.

After Jack found his seat, he caught and held Alaina's gaze for a long, blissful moment. "The great thaw," he quipped in a whisper.

She rolled her eyes and pressed her finger to her lips to shush him from further comment.

Jack engaged her in conversation about the weather, though she noticed he did avoid the usual question of what they would do after service. Charlotte seemed content to make the trip in silence, and Alaina left her to it after her first few attempts to bring her into the conversation failed.

She enjoyed sharing chatter on various subjects with Jack. After the previous night's storm of emotion, he seemed attentive, though circles showed under his eyes. They were engaged in a fiery back-and-forth regarding the chances of the dam breaking when they arrived at the small church.

Frank's children, Missy and Sam, ran up to them.

Jack swung Missy up into his arms and allowed her to perch on his shoulder. "What are you up to this morning, Miss Missy?"

The child giggled at Jack's greeting and beamed at Alaina. "He's silly."

Frank broke through the small crowd, his suspenders worn and his Sunday trousers in sad need of patching. It was on the tip of Alaina's tongue to offer to do the mending when her mother spoke up.

"Frank Willit, what a surprise."

Frank's face lit, and he dipped his head in a shallow bow. "A pleasure to see you, Mrs. Morrison."

"You must bring your mending to me. Missy's dress needs a patch, and I'm sure there is enough material left over from some dresses to make her a new frock."

"And me?" Sam piped up.

Jack scrunched up his face. "You want a dress, Sam?"

Sam cocked his head. "No, why would I want that?"

Jack and Frank guffawed at the boy's confusion.

Charlotte sent them a withering look. "And a pair of pants for you, Sam."

Alaina could only stare at her mother, struck completely dumb, not only by her generous offer but by the interest she showed in the children and Frank. She glanced at Frank and wondered if the big man had captured her mother's fancy. But no, it couldn't be. Charlotte had only met Frank twice before.

Jack let Missy slip to the ground and sidled up next to Alaina as Frank and Charlotte continued their conversation. "Is this the sun coming out?" was Jack's question.

"I—I don't know. I'm as surprised as you are. More so."

Jack chuckled. "Frank's not a bad-looking bloke."

But it didn't explain the sudden change in Charlotte. What had prompted her mother to go from shy and resigned, even bitter, to considerate? Was it simply God's working in her mother's heart? She didn't know, and she wouldn't ask.

When the pastor appeared at the front doors, the group began a mass migration inside.

Jack winked down at Alaina. "I'm going to test the waters. If Frank can be charming, then I can be downright saintly." With that, he strode up to Charlotte.

She glanced his way in time to see his proffered arm. Charlotte hesitated only a moment before accepting, leaving a chagrined Frank standing by himself.

He recovered quickly, though, when his gaze met Alaina's. He copied Jack's gesture and offered his arm, a good-natured grin coloring his cheeks.

She lay her hand lightly on his arm as he tilted his head and whispered, "You watch. Jack's going to win her over."

≈

If Jack's restless night hadn't been unsettling enough, then listening to the sermon on Judas's betrayal and Christ's forgiveness stirred the cauldron of his emotions into full boil. Every word the pastor uttered seemed to stir the same question. *How to forgive betrayal?*

His fidgeting caught Alaina's attention, and only a severe frown from her stilled his quaking limbs. He tried to focus on his plans and ignore the nagging of his spirit, but the pastor continued, now extolling Christ's ability to forgive the unforgivable.

Jack rubbed his hands down his trousers. So many years had passed since his father's failure and death. Did he truly have to forgive a dead man? Wasn't moving on enough? Putting the past behind him and striking out on his own hadn't been easy, but he'd done it. And now he was engaged to Alaina, a beautiful, gentle woman. What would she tell him to do?

What would his mother say? Had she forgiven his father before her death? He tried to remember any conversations he'd had with her in regard to his father and couldn't think of one time when she'd spoken a cross word.

His fingers dug into his palm. Hard. He wanted to believe that she had talked, maybe to others, and blamed Don Kelly for her trouble. It would make Jack's anger toward him easier to deal with.

As the notes of the final hymn lingered in the air, Jack squelched the desire to jump over the pews and burst outside. Instead, he did his duty and waited with everyone else for the pastor to greet his parishioners, one by one.

Alaina kept sending him confused looks, as if trying to diagnose his sudden illness, but the symptoms remained a mystery too hard for her to unravel.

The pastor shook Jack's hand but held on to prevent him from moving along. "You're working hard, Jack. Your face shows your weariness. Unless there is something else troubling you?"

Apparently his fidgeting hadn't gone unnoticed. He could feel Alaina's stare. Shame washed over him. "Your message was quite stirring."

A knowing twinkle flashed in the pastor's eyes. No doubt the man understood evasion when he heard it, but he allowed Jack to pass and turned his attention to Alaina.

Jack waited for her, chagrined when she picked up where

the pastor had left off.

She placed her hand on his arm and leaned toward him ever so slightly. Jack could see the strain of her concern. For him. "This is not about a sleepless night, is it, Jack? It's about last night."

The arrow of her words hit its target. "Let's put it aside and enjoy our afternoon."

Her eyes flashed. "I won't be put off forever."

"I'm not putting you off." He shifted his weight and tried to keep his voice even. "I just don't have anything to tell you."

"You're troubled. You fidgeted more than a wayward boy of five during Pastor's sermon. I think I have a right to know what's troubling you."

"We can talk tomorrow night when I come to visit."

Her dark eyes snapped. "I'm supposed to share in your troubles."

Irritation pricked. "I'm fine."

Alaina's nostrils flared. "Then I'll leave you alone." She jerked around, head held high, and disappeared into the crowd.

Jack rubbed his hand over his brow. Alaina never pushed back, but she'd pushed back this time, and the experience left him shaken.

"Never seen her quite so fired up."

Jack looked over his shoulder to see Frank. "Me neither."

"You going after her?"

"I don't think she wants me to."

Frank's gaze lifted to something over Jack's shoulder. "Well, if you are, you'd better hurry. She and her mother got themselves a ride."

He didn't run after her. There was no use. How had things gone wrong so quickly? The prospect of returning to his dreary place or poring over his plans for a new angle from which to work all seemed hollow now.

ten

May 20, 1889

"Our hero," Clarence Fulton boomed when Jack opened the door of his boss's office.

Jack squinted in the midmorning light coming through the window, clutching his report in one hand. "I came by to drop off my findings on the South Fork Dam."

Mr. Fulton resumed his seat and fixed Jack with a stare that made him cautious. "The clouds are breaking up now." Fulton scooted his chair forward. "Without the rain pouring down, the dam doesn't seem like such a great threat. I'll read over your report. However, I'm more interested right now in that process you're working on."

An edge of irritation made Jack clench his teeth. All that work and now the report meant almost nothing. He made himself concentrate on Fulton's enthusiasm on the other project. "I'm on to something with that. I know it. I'll be working on it today."

"Good. Good. You show great promise, young man. Great promise."

The meeting came to a swift end, and for once, Jack felt relieved to step from his boss's office. As he got closer to the huge room of Open Hearth Furnaces, the temperature spiked, and every footfall became a struggle against his exhaustion. In silence, he watched the men on first shift and empathized with the tedious, dangerous routine of the hot work. As the men bent and shoveled, Jack's muscles echoed the tension and misery so familiar to the job. He strained when they strained, and their shouts quickened his pulse.

He pushed through the doors and out into the light and

cool air. In a corner of the yards that surrounded Cambria, with clear view of Cambria's own railroad depot, Jack rolled up his long sleeves and settled into deep thought about the entire process of converting iron ore into steel. He ran his hand over the miniature egg-shaped Bessemer converter he had shaped from scrap metal and studied his new theory, paying particular attention to the tuyeres through which air was blown to remove impurities from the molten iron. If blasting too much air removed too much carbon, then the resulting product was negatively affected. His new theory worked to solve this problem. With a surge of excitement, he bent his head over his plans.

The work was an elixir. He fell into the rhythm of trial and error, always reviewing the process and tweaking the amount of air blown into the molten iron. Only when he took a break did he allow himself to once again scrape up the discomfort over Alaina's question about his parents—her demand to share what troubled him about his past.

His father.

Jack stared at his hands and realized, ironically, that as much as he detested what his father became as he got older, he had, to a great degree, followed in his father's footsteps. Even as a five-year-old, he recalled being intrigued by his father's passion for creating solutions to problems around their small farm.

But as Jack had gotten older, things had gone wrong. His father kept inventing new and better ways of doing things, but drinking became his new obsession. It took Jack several years to realize that his father's regular drinking companion seldom drank at all. Instead, the man listened to Jack's father's ideas and cashed in on them. Only when the same man stopped giving Jack's father generous stipends did the situation at home become critical and the nightly rages against him and his mother worsened. In the end, he lost both his father and mother within six months of each other.

His mother's agony, the poverty his father had plunged them into by his poor choices, stirred Jack's agony anew as a veil of tears blinded him to the papers in front of him. The pair of pliers he had been using fell from his hand and clinked against a piece of scrap metal. He clenched his fists and swiped at the wetness on his cheeks, struggling against the familiar and bitter hatred his father's memory always stirred.

Pastor's sermon pounded in his head. A bitter Christ would have been useless in God's plan, yet He could have chosen that route. But Jack realized that Christ's decision to hate Judas would have destroyed His life, and the lives of everyone with life and breath.

For him to choose to cling to his bitterness would destroy him just as certainly. He knew it as sure as he knew he was close to a major discovery in his plans.

But how to forgive? He didn't know.

The sound of the whistle signaling the end of the shift and the beginning of another helped shake Jack back to the project at hand. His hand trembled as he pulled another sheet of paper from the pocket of his trousers and spread it out next to the others. He forced himself to focus on comparing his old notes with his new. After reviewing everything, he decided to tinker with the idea of heating the molten iron longer, lowering the impurities. Then...

His blood pumped hard through his veins as a chill shock snapped through him. If he could lower the impurities by heating longer and reintroduce...

Jack swallowed hard and made furious notes as the idea unfolded in his mind. Throughout his shift he reviewed the process over and over. By the time he arrived home that night, his excitement had faded into a bone-weary tiredness that made his muscles ache. He bypassed eating and did only as much as necessary to prepare for the next morning, when he would arrive earlier than necessary so he could work on this new angle.

Satisfied, he stretched out on his cot and pulled the blanket up over his shoulders. As he lay there, his mind caught between sleep and wakefulness, Jack remembered Alaina. Her smile, her concern, her anger. . .his promise to see her.

For a minute he hung in a semiconscious state, disgusted at how he could forget so easily. Again. But his weary mind and body pulled him down into a black oblivion he had no strength to fight.

Alaina will understand.

eleven

May 21, 1889

"Don't pour!" Jack's scream rent the air seconds before the molten steel touched the water in the steel-mold.

An explosion rocked the men not already undercover back on their heels.

Jack skidded into a low crouch and shielded his face. A blast of strong, hot air choked him and scorched his skin. Chunks of metal shot around the room, and Jack heard the muffled groan of pain next to him that told him Big Frank had been hit.

When the air settled, the factory whistle screamed the news of another accident to all within listening distance. Shouts lifted above the sounds of machinery as other men went to the rescue of those downed by the explosion.

Jack jumped up and hustled over to where Frank lay within a few feet of the mold. Still. Silent.

"God, no. God, please, no." He flipped Big Frank over. His heart plummeted at the sight of blood. Frank's shirt smoked where the heat had singed the material. "Frank? Frank!" He patted his friend's cheek, strangled with dread when Frank remained unresponsive. He lifted his head. "Help! Over here."

Someone appeared at his side, and together they lifted the big man and carried him away from the heat of the open hearth furnaces.

⁂

Hospital beds lined both walls of the long room. Frank lay, pale and bandaged, eyes closed, halfway down the long room.

Jack recognized other workers and waved a greeting to those who were awake.

One of the men, Sweeney, as everyone called him, returned

Jack's greeting with a grim, "How many this time?"

"Three." Jack stopped and ran a cautious eye over the man's bandaged arm and chest. "Three died. Five injured."

Sweeney rubbed at the bandage on his arm, then grimaced. "Hurt's like fire, but it's a graze."

"You were blessed not to have been killed."

The man leaned back against his pillow and gave a nod.

Jack headed down the row toward Frank and stopped at the foot of his friend's bed. He bowed his head, grateful Frank's life had been spared.

He lifted his face to find Frank's glazed stare upon him. "Not dead, am I? Was thinkin' God had allowed some pretty ugly angels to mess up heaven."

Jack's breath released in a relieved gust. He laughed and moved to the side of the bed. "Hey there. How're you feeling?"

"Like a piece of hot slag got me in the gut."

"And the face." Jack felt the burn of guilt. "If I hadn't left, it would have spared you from doing the pouring and getting hit."

Frank blinked slowly. "God orders the day, son. Haven't you figured that out yet? No amount of guilt is going to change the way things happen."

It took a minute for Jack to gain his voice. He gripped Frank's hand. "What about Missy and Sam?"

Frank seemed to drift off to a faraway place for a moment. Then his eyes fixed on the ceiling. "I don't know. Mrs. Sanford can't keep them. Too old."

"I'll do it. I'll take care of them for you, Frank. Alaina is home from the lake. She can watch them during the day and I'll help her in the evenings."

"You've got work to do, boy. Riches to make. An invention to invent."

Jack could hear the hopeful note behind Frank's playful words. "Then it's settled. Alaina won't mind, I know it. She loves Missy and Sam."

"You've a good heart, Jack."

"You concentrate on getting better."

❧

After Sunday, then forgetting about Alaina the night before, Jack felt every bit the fool for arriving on her doorstep with two children in tow.

She opened the door immediately, and his anxiousness lifted at her look of pleased surprise.

"Why, Missy and Sam, what are you doing here?"

Missy promptly broke into tears, and Sam shushed her.

Alaina met Jack's gaze with a question.

He leaned forward and whispered in her ear.

She gasped in dismay, then stooped to take first Missy's hand and then Sam's and led them inside.

Jack swept the room for any sign of Alaina's mother.

"She's not here. She's downstairs finishing up an order due tomorrow." Alaina pulled young Missy onto her lap and wiped her tears. She cuddled the six-year-old close and smoothed her ruffled hair.

Jack placed his hand on Missy's head. "How about I go downstairs and get some candy?"

Alaina gave him a searching look.

He winked and crouched to whisper into Missy's ear. "I need someone to help me pick. Want to come?"

Missy's solemn, gray gaze stirred something in his heart. "Will my daddy die?"

Jack rasped a hand down his unshaven cheek. Other than his initial fear that Frank had been outright killed, he hadn't considered his friend might die from his injuries. Frank was older than most of the men, at thirty-three years, but his strength would be in his favor. But to offer the child hope and have things take a turn for the worse. . .

Jack picked up Missy's small hand and got eye level with her. "I can't answer that question. No one can. But we can pray and trust and ask God to help us as we wait. Would you like to do that with me?"

"And Sam and Miss Alaina?"

"Sure."

Missy scrambled off Alaina's lap and dropped to her knees. Sam joined her. Jack and Alaina shared an amused look over the small heads. Missy tucked her hands together and looked at the ceiling. Jack got the feeling the child saw far beyond the stained plaster. Maybe even into the heart of God.

"Do you want to pray, Missy?"

She shook her head and pointed to him.

The words came easily to Jack. When he said, "Amen," he took the little girl into his arms, where her confidence failed her and she sobbed.

Sam stood nearby, tears trailing a silver streak down his pudgy face. Alaina settled a hand on the boy's shoulder.

"Will Mrs. Sanford watch us until Daddy is better?" Missy's words muffled against his shirt.

Jack swallowed hard. "I was hoping Miss Alaina might spend some time with you while your father recovers." His eyes pleaded with Alaina. "Your father said Mrs. Sanford was too old to watch you both full time."

He hesitated under Alaina's steady gaze, ashamed to be asking her for a favor when so much still stood between them. *I'm sorry*, he mouthed to her.

She didn't smile, but her eyes traced along Missy's back then over Sam's head and down to his shoes. Her expression softened. "We can make a place for you two on the floor in my room."

Sam hugged her legs, and Missy smiled shyly up at her.

Jack got to his feet. "Why don't the two of you head down to the store and check out that candy display."

"You want to kiss her?" Missy wanted to know. Her nose wrinkled as if the thought disgusted her.

Jack laughed. "You think that's so bad?"

"Daddy kissed Mommy a whole lot," she continued. "He loved her." With that, she turned and headed down the steps.

"Hold on to the railing," Alaina called after them.

He caught her gaze. "Maybe a better question is, would Miss Alaina even allow me to kiss her?"

twelve

The weight of Jack's question caused her to hesitate. Always she was so quick to forgive him for breaking his word to her. What had it earned her? "I don't know, Jack." She couldn't bear to return his stare or to see the hurt in his eyes and stared down after Missy and Sam instead. "We'd better go after the children."

"Alaina, wait." His hand encased her wrist, but she refused to turn. He rested his hands lightly on her shoulders, his words placating. "I got another idea for the converter and began work on it. I lost track of the time. I'm sorry."

She felt the warmth of his breath against her cheek.

"I thought you would understand."

Her throat grew thick, and she stared at him as tears collected in her eyes. "Why don't you try to understand how *I* feel for a change? How it feels to be forgotten by the man who says he loves you and wants to marry you. Not once, Jack. Not twice—" The tears rolled, and her voice caught. "Try ten times. Maybe twenty. You always say it's for us, for *me*. But I don't care about money, don't you see? It's you, Jack. Money is *your* issue, not mine. I'm *happy* being poor. *People* are more important than things. And then, when I want to help you, to reach out to the man I love and share what is obviously troubling him, I'm turned away."

His hands slid down her arms then released her.

Unable to stand it any longer, she hurried down the steps, drying her eyes as she went, not wanting her mother to have further reason to be upset with Jack. As she stepped through the back door of the store, her mother glanced up.

Charlotte set her sewing aside and rubbed her eyes. "I saw the children come in from the back door. Is Big Frank visiting?"

"You should stop for the night, Mother. It's not good for your eyes to work such long hours."

Charlotte waved a hand in dismissal of her concern. "I'm paid well to have these gowns done quickly. The money is worth the long hours." She stretched her neck from side to side, her eyes flicking toward the entrance that led to the front of the store. "Now how did those two come to be here?"

"Jack brought them over." Her mother's lips curved down into a frown, and Alaina hastened to continue. "Cambria had an accident today. Frank's in the hospital."

Charlotte's face drained of color. "Oh no."

"The children need a place to stay, so Jack thought I could watch them during the day while he's at work."

Her mother's mouth tightened. "Did he think to *ask* first?"

"It happened so suddenly—"

Charlotte's eyes flashed. "Stop it, Alaina. Stop defending him. I can't stand to see you hurt by him."

The door behind Alaina creaked open, and she knew without looking that it was Jack.

"Good evening, Mrs. Morrison."

Charlotte tilted her head in acknowledgment of Jack's greeting, but her lips remained pressed into a grim line.

Alaina nodded toward the front of the store. "Why don't you check on the children, Jack?"

Charlotte resumed her seat and repositioned the material around her legs. "I've got to get this dress finished."

Jack remained glued to the spot. "Since I have to work, I wanted to know if it would be all right for Sam and Missy to spend the day with Alaina. There was a bad accident today. Frank got hit real bad."

Charlotte jammed her needle into the material and pulled through the other side. "So Alaina tells me. But it's not my decision. It's up to Alaina."

"Mother, Jack's trying to be polite."

"I would consider it polite if he didn't bother me with questions that don't need my answer."

Jack flinched. "I don't know what I've done to deserve your hostility, Mrs. Morrison, but whatever it is, I'm sorry."

Charlotte's head shot up. "Just like you're sorry for all those times you haven't shown up to take Alaina on a picnic, or roller-skating, or for a stroll? That kind of sorry is a word with no meaning."

A muscle jumped in Jack's jaw. "I can understand how you must feel that way, but I assure you, Mrs. Morrison, that I work very hard only in hopes of providing for Alaina in a way befitting to the woman I hope to marry." He turned toward Alaina, as if seeking some measure of support.

It was there on her tongue to assure her mother that she understood and didn't hold it against Jack, but it struck her that putting voice to such sentiments would be a lie. A lie she had perpetrated to give Jack peace, all the while allowing her own to slip away.

"You want to believe that, Jack Kelly. But I've been where Alaina is now. You cannot blame me for instilling in her a need for caution against marrying you, when you mistreat her as much as you do."

Jack's face flushed, and Alaina, afraid of drawing attention to themselves should Jack choose to continue the argument, grabbed his hand and tugged. "Let's leave. Now."

To her relief, Jack acknowledged her request with a stiff nod but turned once more toward her mother. "I know you are right in many ways, but I have seen the other side of poverty and know the strain it puts on a person's mind. I want to avoid putting that kind of strain on my wife."

Charlotte did not respond, though the quick stab at the material let Alaina know her mother had indeed heard.

❧

Jack called to Missy and Sam as he followed Alaina to the front of the store. The children bolted toward him and held up the candy sticks. Peppermint for both Missy and Sam. He smiled and feigned interest in their chatter, not hearing much more than the ring of first Alaina's and then Charlotte's verbal attacks.

The children sucked happily as they went up the big steps. Jack held back. "I'll wait here."

Alaina followed the children upstairs. "I'll settle them and be back down."

Beside the big maple tree, Jack rehearsed what he would tell Alaina. It would cheer her to learn that he'd be turning in his final papers to Mr. Fulton soon, freeing him to spend more time with her and the children. It would put her fears to rest. And Charlotte's.

The streetlamps flickered in the dark, and drops of rain forced Jack to take shelter under the maple's spreading branches. No matter what he did, it never seemed right.

"Jack?"

When he faced her, she stood in the shadow of the branches. He captured her hand and turned her until the lamplight highlighted her expression. Strain and worry marked the areas around her eyes and mouth.

Shame washed over him, and his heart twisted for the pain Alaina's eyes reflected. "I've made a mess of things."

Alaina stayed silent, and her silence put a weight in his stomach. "I should have told your mother that I'd be turning in the papers to Mr. Fulton in only a few days. Then I'll be done."

"That is good news." Her voice lacked conviction.

"It'll mean we can spend more time together. It's only that I've been so distracted by everything. You know how much it means to me to take good care of you, Alaina."

"Jack. . ."

He barely heard her as the feeling that she was slipping away from him grew. Panic surged and he clasped her hand tighter, begging with his words as much as his heart for her to understand.

She pulled her hand away. "What happens when something else 'distracts' you? Is this why you're so angry with your father? Did he do this to you?"

"He was an inventor, yes. But we can talk about him some other time."

"No. No, Jack. I want you to tell me about your father."

The gentle command slashed through his fears and stabbed coldness into his heart, and Jack understood, in that moment, both the depth of his bitterness toward Don Kelly and how much he needed to forgive his father. He gulped air. "He's dead."

Alaina flattened her hand against his until their palms met. He watched as she traced the outline of his knuckles with her fingers.

The motion soothed him. Seconds stretched into minutes and Jack grew calmer, more clearheaded.

When she finally met his gaze, her smile was beatific and gentle. "He hurt you."

He closed his eyes as the emotion welled up again, threatening to drown him.

"Tell me, Jack."

With a hard exhale, he made up his mind. Riding the crest of his anger and frustration, grief and sorrow, he told Alaina about his father. And his mother. The farm. The drinking. The lack of money. His father's death. . .

"He was sick?" she asked.

Jack pressed his lips together to stop the trembling.

"Jack?" She moved in close to him and peered up into his face.

He could not look away from those eyes. Didn't want to.

"How did your father die?"

He struggled to draw air into his lungs. "Mama found him." He closed his eyes against the image that greeted them that morning in the barn. His mother had been out before him, then had come racing back to get him, eyes wild. Hair mussed. Out of breath.

Jack took a step away from Alaina. Then another. Until his back touched the tall maple tree.

"Oh, Jack," he heard Alaina's words through a haze of pain and anguish.

In his mind he saw again the flash of light against the blade of the knife as it winked before he cut through the rope that held the weight of his father's body.

God, help me.

Jack's legs went weak, and he felt himself plunging downward, his shirt catching on the rough bark of the maple.

And Alaina was there beside him. Holding him tight.

"He hung himself, Lainey. He. . ."

Her hand stroked his head as the tears streamed down his face.

thirteen

In the weak morning light filtering through her window, Alaina felt the pull of a thousand emotions. She lay as still as possible, praying the children wouldn't wake so she might have time to sort through her feelings before helping them get dressed for the day. She focused on a spot on the ceiling and sank into prayer, laying all her struggles at God's feet. Silent tears slipped from her eyes as she reviewed everything that had occurred in the last few days and the terrible secret Jack had revealed. She prayed God would heal his heart.

Learning of Don Kelly's death had left her breathless with hurt for Jack. Her admiration of him had gone up a notch, just as the knowledge of all that he'd faced as an orphan had sketched a greater empathy for him in her heart. It had cost him so much to share with her his private shame, for she knew that his father's suicide had been a wrenching grief that wouldn't heal.

When Jack's tears had finally stopped, she had helped him to his feet and scrambled for something to say, but Sam had chosen that moment to open the door and holler down for her. She'd been torn then, wanting to give Jack the reassurance he so needed, but the sound of Missy's crying forced her to choose.

Jack's gentle shove and his whispered, "I've got to get back anyway," had helped.

She'd hesitated long enough to rise on her toes and touch her lips to his cheek before rushing up the steps, saddened to see the slump of his shoulders as his steps took him away from her.

That had been two days ago.

She worried over his extended absence yet knew instinctively that he would drive himself to finish his work for Mr. Fulton until it was completed. But it wasn't fair to Missy and Sam. They were growing restless and worried about their father.

She couldn't help but see that it was one more time when people meant less to Jack than his drive to have money. Now, though, she understood the basis for his drive to succeed. On one hand, she still felt slighted by him, but on the other, she understood how growing up poor and watching his father lose everything, drink by drink, had scarred him.

Alaina wanted so much for God to give her peace about her relationship with Jack. His approval. It seemed like all opposition had been unleashed on them since their engagement. An involuntary shiver made her teeth click. She wiped the moisture from her face and tried to dissolve the gripping knot of fear in the pit of her stomach. More than God's direct answer, she feared His silence.

Sam stirred and bounced to his feet, balled fists working at the sleep in his eyes.

Alaina had to smile at his display of enthusiasm for the day. "Good morning, Sam. Did you sleep well?"

He blinked around the room, his gaze settling on her. He gave her a solemn nod and poked at Missy. The girl grunted. Her hair spilled out behind her along the pillow next to Alaina. By the looks of the curls, it would take quite a while to get the tangles worked free.

Within minutes, Missy, too, bounded to her feet and began a stream of chatter as she dressed.

"Missy, stand still so I can button you," Alaina admonished the girl.

"I have to go out," Sam said. "*Now.*"

Freed from Alaina's ministrations, Missy reached to snap Sam's suspenders into place. "I'm ready."

Alaina showed the children from her room and pulled on her day dress. They made short work of the trip to the outhouse and reentered to find her mother working on breakfast. Alaina leaned in to plant a kiss on her mother's cheek.

"Miss Alaina," Missy popped around her elbow. "Sam has dirt all around."

"Well, it sounds like Sam needs to wash up. Let me get some water heated."

"I can take care of myself!" Sam stormed at his sister. "Stop bossing, Missy."

Alaina silenced Missy's reply, "Let's try not to fight." She put Missy to work setting the table as the water heated.

Charlotte served up the oatmeal with a grim smile for each of the children and a kiss on the top of Alaina's head.

"I want some syrup," Missy declared.

Alaina fetched the can and allowed each a spoonful of brown sugar and a dollop of syrup. The soothing scent of the maple and the velvet texture of the oatmeal soothed Alaina and helped her focus.

"Why hasn't Jack told us about Daddy?" Missy asked.

Alaina gestured for the girl to eat and shook her head. "Jack has to work, just like your father would have to work if he were feeling better."

Missy scooped up another spoonful and aimed it at her mouth, but one more question slipped out. "Will Daddy lose his job? Mark Rosenfelt's daddy lost his job after he hurt his hand."

"I don't know, Missy. Why don't we make it a matter of prayer?"

Charlotte remained quiet through the meal but spoke up as Missy scraped the last of the oatmeal from her bowl. "Why don't you help me, Sam, while Miss Alaina helps Missy get cleaned up?"

The boy nodded and shoveled in the last bite.

Alaina smiled her gratitude at her mother and took Missy to her room. She brushed the gnarls out of the long, wheat-colored hair and braided it to prevent further tangles.

"My mother used to do the same thing." Missy yawned into her hand.

Alaina's fingers stilled. It was too easy to forget how much grief Missy and Sam had already experienced in their young lives. She closed her eyes and forced away the last vestiges of her own melancholy, remembering an oft-stated phrase of her old Sunday school teacher.

"Those who too often look inward, seldom look upward."

No matter the problems she might have, Sam and Missy needed her full attention.

જ

Jack stopped at his place long enough to clean up before heading over to Alaina's. They had reason to celebrate. He'd pulled a lot of long hours between his job, working to prove his theory, and checking on Frank, but his burden had lifted considerably when he'd passed his plans to Mr. Fulton during a break in his shift.

Clarence Fulton had stroked his face as he read over the papers, and when he'd raised his eyes to Jack's, his smile had been huge. "I think you're on to something. Let me pass these up to someone who would know more about such things, and we'll get back to you." Clarence squinted at the calendar on his desk. "We should hear something back by the end of the month, I'd say. How does that sound?"

Elation had carried Jack through the rest of the long, hot shift and all the way home. As he splashed water onto his face to soothe his hot skin, he felt buoyed by thoughts of the time he would get to spend with Alaina. And Sam and Missy, of course. He combed his hair in the small mirror over his shaving stand, noting his need for a trim, then snapped his suspenders into place.

When he arrived at the dispensary to check on Frank's condition, the edge of his happiness faded somewhat. Frank's skin was flushed with fever.

When Frank saw Jack, he waved him over. "Miss the mites. They behaving themselves?"

Jack grinned. "Hello to you, too."

Frank grunted. "You have any idea what it's like lying flat on your back like this?"

"I wish I did."

Frank frowned. "Don't talk foolish."

Jack hitched his chair closer to the edge of Frank's bedside. "I see you're not feeling well."

"Doc says the fever could kill me or make me better. Sobering words." Frank's jaw worked, and his Adam's apple bobbed. "I'm all Sam and Missy have, Jack."

"You'll pull through this. Only the good die young."

His friend scowled. "Then you'll surely outlive me by a few centuries."

Jack laughed.

The levity shattered Frank's scowl and seemed to improve his temperament. "I really appreciate Alaina watching Missy and Sam for me."

"You know how much she loves children."

Frank threw off his thin blanket. "You'd better make that woman yours soon, or someone else is liable to claim her."

Jack clamped his hands together. "Sooner rather than later, I'm hoping. If I get this promotion, we'll be set."

"Promotion or not. . ." Frank's brows lowered. "Why you looking so smug?"

"Congratulate me. I just turned in the papers stating my theory to Mr. Fulton. I'm on to something, Frank. It's really going to work."

Instead of words of praise, Frank gave him a hard look. "You're not listening to me, boy. Get your head off invention. Lying here's made me think about a whole lot. You included. And I'm telling you, you'd be better off with Alaina than with anything a promotion or that invention will get you." Frank shifted and winced, his face losing some color, his voice roughened from pain. "Be glad when the burns heal up and these ribs let me draw in a decent breath."

"I'll bring Missy and Sam by. They'll be glad to see you."

"How long's it been since you saw them?"

Frank's question brought a surge of anger. "A while. I had some work to do and—"

"Tell them I miss them and I love them."

Jack could see the tension in Frank's face and body and knew his friend must be in a great deal more pain than he allowed others to see, but it didn't give him a right to try and tell him what to do.

Frank grimaced. "Even Alaina?"

"Alaina what?"

"Tell her you love her. Daily, Jack. Time's too short."

Jack winced at the sharp edge of rebuke in Frank's tone.

"She's too precious to be ignored."

"I don't ignore her."

Frank's eyes burned into his. "You mean, you don't think you do."

fourteen

Jack bounded up the steps to Alaina's. Laughter spilled through the closed door, putting a smile on his lips. He almost hated to knock and interrupt the flow of joy. A high-pitched squeal rent the air, followed by another, and he imagined Alaina chasing Sam and Missy, as he had witnessed her play with the Hensley children so many times. Longing to be a part of the scene, he knocked, and the door opened to reveal the wide smile of Charlotte Morrison. "Mrs. Morrison," he nodded and held his breath as he watched her smile wither and her eyes lose the luster of joy.

"You're here for the children?" She neither opened the door in invitation nor slammed it in his face.

He exhaled. "I thought Alaina might walk with me for a bit."

Charlotte stared back over her shoulder, then retreated enough for him to see Alaina crossing the room as she worked to untie her apron. He didn't miss the warning glance Alaina gave her mother. For her part, Mrs. Morrison seemed resigned, more than angered, by Jack's arrival.

"I'll ready the children and meet you outside," Alaina directed him. She yanked the apron over her head and brushed back a few tendrils of hair that had pulled loose.

He retreated a step and nodded. "I'll be here."

It only took a few minutes before she appeared with the children. She had changed from her work dress into her best blue, worn patches evident around the elbows and cuffs. How he wanted to purchase an entire new wardrobe for her for a wedding gift. Alaina's eyes would shine with excitement and delight over the materials. She could have all the ruffles and frills, bustles and trains she wanted.

The children ran straight to the maple tree and began to

give chase. When Alaina came level with him on the last step, he captured her hand in his. The coolness of her skin sent a spark of awareness through him.

"I have good news. I turned in the papers to Mr. Fulton today."

They turned when Missy squealed. Sam jumped out at his sister again, and Missy screamed with fright.

Alaina laughed, her eyes on the children, but Jack couldn't take his eyes off her. When she caught his gaze, something flared in the depths of her burgundy-brown eyes. "They're as happy to play as I am to hear your good news. We can set a date."

"Mr. Fulton said I should know by the end of the month, and I'm sure the announcement about the promotion will be soon. We'll set a date after I know more. We'll be financially secure."

The spark in her eyes lost its luster. "Of course. We'll wait."

Jack released a frustrated breath at the flat tone in her voice.

Missy chose that moment to barrel into Alaina. The child pressed her face into the folds of Alaina's skirts. Missy remained there only a few seconds before beckoned by her brother to play chase again.

Alaina watched the children circle the maple. "I think Mother is actually enjoying their presence," she murmured. "You should have seen the way she carried on with them before you arrived."

"Perhaps grandchildren will endear her to me if nothing else will." Jack tried to keep his tone light.

Alaina gasped and glanced at him, then away. Fire flamed in her cheeks.

Maybe he was playing the fool thinking he could wait to marry Alaina. She often said how content she would be to be poor. . . . But when his mind skittered to the leaky roof and mice in his sad shack to his mother's final days, surrounded by dirt and filth and wearing rags, he knew he would have to bide his time. He lifted his face to the sun and tried to reabsorb the lightheartedness he'd felt upon arrival. "Why don't we go for a picnic in the mountains?"

"A picnic?" Missy, closest to them, stopped so fast she slipped on the rain-soaked grass.

Sam stooped to help her up. "A picnic?" But his expression was anxious.

Jack didn't understand Sam's reaction and lifted an eyebrow at Alaina.

Alaina held his gaze. "Isn't there somewhere else we should go?"

He caught the direction of her thoughts and gave Sam's hair a tousle. "Sure. We'll eat, and then we'll go by and see your papa. How's that sound?"

But Sam didn't respond. He stared off into the distance. Missy drew closer to her brother.

"I think we should save the picnic for later," Alaina suggested. *They're worried*, she mouthed to him.

Jack acquiesced. "To the hospital then."

❧

When they arrived, they were told Frank was sleeping and they could not visit. A nurse did tell Jack that Frank's fever had broken. A good sign, she had assured them.

Missy and Sam sagged in disappointment at not being able to see their father.

Alaina hoped the picnic would put a sparkle back into their eyes.

Jack, seeming to sense the importance of diverting Missy and Sam's attention, grabbed their hands and began chattering about visiting the grocer to buy candy. "But first..." Jack's hand snaked out and tousled Sam's hair. He withdrew and, quick as a wink, lunged back into a boxer's crouch, hands fisted.

The boy responded to the fun immediately and let out a flailing, sloppy right hook that Jack easily blocked.

Alaina watched the fun with amusement.

Missy rolled her eyes and planted her little hands on

nonexistent hips. "I'm hungry."

Jack dove in toward Sam and caught the boy around his waist. He raised the boy over his shoulder and winked at Alaina. "Well, now that Sam is out of the way, I guess there'll be more for us to eat. Right, Missy?"

Sam squawked and began to kick his feet in protest.

Jack laughed and let the boy slide to the ground.

Nothing could hide the shine of joy in Sam's eyes, and Alaina was reminded, again, how much she loved Jack's fun side. If only she could lift the burden of his need for the promotion or to make the invention that would line his pockets with the money he so desperately wanted to lavish on her. No matter how many times she stated her contentment, it seemed to fall on deaf ears.

Alaina combed her fingers through Sam's mussed hair, but the boy grimaced and pulled back.

"Best let her spiff you up, Sam. Women like to do that sort of thing."

Alaina cocked an eyebrow at him. "Oh?" She let her gaze slide over Jack's hair. A sudden longing to straighten the lock flopped on his forehead brought immediate heat to her cheeks.

He noticed. "Do I need spiffing?"

She raised her chin. "I'm sure you do, but I'll not be the one doing it."

Jack leaned in close to her ear. "A shame. I'll make sure not to be spiffed when we marry. Then you can spend the day getting me straightened out."

She gasped and felt the receding heat of her previous blush flare back full force. But she couldn't quite quell the tingle of excitement his outrageous comment stirred. To be his wife. Her heart raced with the thrill of it.

Her gaze caught his and held. She felt herself wrapped in the warmth of his blue eyes. A small smile crooked the corners of his mouth. His hand closed over her forearm and slipped down to cradle hers. When he lowered his head a fraction, she tilted her head back even more. The touch of his lips brought a sigh to her throat.

"Yuck!"

Alaina's eyes flew open.

Jack's face, so close to hers, split into a huge grin, and he turned toward a disgruntled Sam. "Oh yes, little man, you should try it sometime," Jack admonished Sam with a playful swipe at the boy's shoulder.

"When you're much older," Alaina added, sending a warning look at Jack.

Jack's head jerked back, and he released a stream of hearty laughter.

Alaina stamped her foot and crossed her arms. "Jack Kelly, you're incorrigible."

He brushed the hair from his forehead and shrugged. "Got to teach him what courting a beautiful woman is all about."

Missy pulled on Jack's free hand. "Momma used to do that to Papa. It makes me miss her."

"I didn't mean to make you sad, Missy." He squinted up at the sky. "Why don't we get to picnicking before it rains again?"

fifteen

Taking Alaina out always filled Jack with great satisfaction. They visited the grocer, and he dipped into his hoarded fund of coins to purchase candy for the children and apples, cheese, and a bit of bread for everyone.

He watched how Alaina interacted with others they met along the walk to the hill, both strangers and friends, and never failed to find himself endeared to her all the more for her kindness and gentleness of spirit. He found himself wondering how Charlotte Morrison could raise a child with a temperament so contrary to her own. But he knew life's disappointments had dealt a blow to Charlotte that had shaped the person she'd become. Frank had been right. He must keep that in mind, though sometimes it was hard. Even harder to comprehend was the idea that Alaina might suffer a disappointment because of him. End up poor and miserable. He clenched his jaw. Not if he could help it.

When they settled the blanket on the ground, she spread out the meager meal, and Jack felt hot shame. There should be more food. More candy for the children. Alaina should have better clothes. . . .

She sent him a questioning look from her place next to young Missy, and Jack felt the sudden pressure of time being wasted. Perhaps he should go over his notes again. Though he'd turned his theory over to Mr. Fulton, he couldn't keep at bay the nagging fear that he'd forgotten something. By the slant of the sun, he knew he had little time left in the day to review his plans before his shift started. He swept to his feet, threw his apple core far out into the tall grass, and stretched.

Missy helped Alaina gather the remaining scraps of bread. She showed Missy how to tear the pieces into smaller bits and then scatter them for the birds. The child watched in wide-eyed wonder as a single cardinal floated down and hopped closer and closer, his bright little eyes on a good-sized crumb.

Jack couldn't help but smile at the child's delight.

Alaina sidled close and whispered, "I'm worried about Sam."

The boy was nowhere to be seen. "Where'd he go?" Jack asked.

She pointed to the edge of the woods, where Jack caught a glimpse of Sam's dark head among a thicket of tall grass. "I think he's worried about his father."

Jack rubbed his forehead. He could well understand the boy's concern and felt the claw of doubt scratch at his own mind when he considered Frank's condition. "I'll go talk to him, but I have to get back to town." He caught Alaina's gaze. "I can't stop this feeling that I overlooked something in my notes."

He held his breath, hoping for her understanding. A sharp chill shot through him when Alaina, instead, turned away, back ramrod straight. He reached out a hand to turn her toward him but let it drop back to his side when his tongue found no words to console.

He stepped around her and focused on retrieving Sam, but every footfall fanned the embers of his anger. Why couldn't she understand? Didn't his time with her this afternoon show how much he cared? The tender kiss and the smoky look in her eyes had seemed so full of promise for their future. Yet every time he mentioned the project, it seemed to build a wall between them.

When Jack reached the spot where he'd last seen Sam, he stopped and squinted into the tall grass. The boy sat far away from his original location, feet dangling just above the shorter grass under the fallen log upon which he had perched.

"Sam? It's time to go. We've got to head back to town."

Sam didn't raise his face, though a curt nod of his head acknowledged he'd heard. He slipped off the log, feet dragging with every step.

When he got within reach, Jack pulled the boy close. He pressed the back of Sam's head against his side and swallowed hard over the knot of emotion swelling in his own throat. Under his hand, he felt the first shudder of the boy's narrow shoulders. He knelt in the tall grass to get eye level with Sam. "You're afraid for your father?"

A small, quiet sob shook the boy's chest. "Will he—" Sam sucked in a shuddering breath. "Will he go away like Momma?"

How much Jack wished he could give the boy solid reassurance, but he understood the extent of Frank's injuries and knew the days ahead would play heavily on whether or not Sam's father would recover. Yet Sam wanted someone to tell him no. To drive away the merciless bats of fear beating their wings against his fragile peace of mind.

Jack dragged in a deep breath and grasped the boy's heaving shoulders. "I don't know, Sam. I do know that your father is badly hurt but that he's strong and wants to live so he can take care of you and Missy."

"He said Momma dying was for the best. Does God think taking him will be for the best, too?"

Jack's eyes squeezed shut at the rawness of that question. He pulled Sam into his embrace and spread his hand on the boy's small back, while the memory of himself as a young boy being embraced by his father after a fall washed over him. Jack swallowed hard and, for the first time, let himself grieve for that part of his father that he'd loved and trusted.

Sam tugged on his sleeve. "Are you sad about Papa?"

Jack ran the back of his hand across the wetness on his cheeks. "Yes. Very. He is my friend, Sam. A very good friend."

sixteen

May 29, 1889

"Well, Jack-o, guess you'll have to get used to calling me 'sir' now." Robert Whitfield's triumphant expression came into sharp focus.

Jack's spine stiffened. Rage began a slow boil.

The promotion.

After all the grunt work he'd done for Fulton. . .all his plans and hopes dashed.

"No worries, though." Robert bared his teeth. "I'll be a good shift manager. The boss has a lot of confidence in me. More than in others."

Jack saw the bait dangled before him. Robert clamped a hand on Jack's shoulder, outwardly looking like a friendly gesture, but Jack felt the unnecessary pressure and schooled his features not to show any pain.

"I'll look forward to working as your boss. But I warn you now. . .I don't tolerate those who don't do their jobs."

Jack clenched his fists, hoping his glare would stab a hole in Robert's cockiness. His thoughts splintered. How could he tell Alaina the news? He would never be able to afford marriage now. He would be forced to break their engagement. But how could he do that?

Robert took a step back. "Since I get off before you, I'll deliver the good news to Alaina. She'll want to know, right?"

Jack forced himself not to react as Robert gave his shoulder a pat and sauntered off. He had no doubt the man would be on Alaina's doorstep within an hour, gloating, and he could do nothing about it.

He worked fast and hard during his shift. Images of Robert

arriving on Alaina's doorstep haunted him. He picked up his pace and shoveled harder. Faster.

"You're gonna kill yourself, Jack." He heard Frank's voice in his head.

Thoughts of his friend's condition, of his inability to care for his family, helped bring perspective to Jack's problems. At least he could still earn a wage. He was unharmed and strong, and he could still hope Mr. Fulton found his theory worthy.

When the greaser came along to oil the machinery, Jack breathed in relief and made his way through the room to the outside. Rain sprinkled down on his face, cooling his body.

More rain. Little Conemaugh bore none of a resemblance to its name now. It raged and slurped at the banks, barely containing its swelling girth. Jack considered what the constant rain was doing to the South Fork Dam. If the Little Conemaugh roared like this, the streams feeding into Lake Conemaugh would be swollen as well, in turn pushing the lake higher and higher toward the crest of the dam.

Only a handful of people seemed worried about the structure. Too many years of crying wolf had cauterized most of Johnstown's population's ability to see the dam as a real threat.

But the knowledge he'd gleaned in his research for Mr. Fulton weighed on him. His already exhausted limbs stiffened with fear. *God, if that dam goes, we're all dead.*

Losing Alaina would be devastating, whether losing her to Robert or to floodwaters. He couldn't let either happen.

When he opened the door to his room, a thin, steady stream of water cascaded from the roof. He emptied the smaller pot of its store of rainwater and placed a bigger pot underneath the growing hole in the roof.

What he needed most was a bath. He smiled at the absurdity of taking a bath when all he needed to do was stand outside with a bar of soap to get the job done. But mirth fizzled when Robert's leering grin popped into his head.

❧

"You'd be happier with him."

Alaina pressed the palms of her hands against her eyes. No matter what she did or said, her mother's words kept pecking at her love for Jack. Robert's visit, though short and to the point, hadn't helped matters, and her mother overhearing Robert's news that he'd received the promotion instead of Jack only added fuel to her argument.

"Robert is the kind of man that will do something with his life. If you're not careful, you'll lose him to Mary. You can bet she has her eyes on him."

"Mary is my friend," Alaina reminded her mother.

"Friend or not. . ."

Alaina felt the tension stretch along her nerves. She knew what her mother's next attack would be.

"At least go to Pittsburgh and look the college over. Give yourself some time away from here to clear your head."

Alaina let her hands fall to the table. "Meaning, away from Jack."

Charlotte's lips tightened into a firm line, and she squinted harder at the needle poking through the hem of the gown she had been working on all evening. "Away from Jack is not a bad place to be."

"Why do you hate Jack so much?" There, she'd asked the question that had nagged at her for so long.

Charlotte set aside her sewing, her expression stricken. "It's not that I hate him, Alaina. Jack's a nice young man. But why can't you wait a while to marry? Consider going to college. If he wants to marry you, won't he wait? Doesn't he want what's best for you?"

Missy appeared at Alaina's elbow, hair mussed and tears welling in her eyes. "Sam pulled my hair."

Welcoming the intrusion, Alaina went to where Sam sat on the floor rolling an empty spool back and forth between his hands. She sank to the floor, her skirt billowing out around her, and slipped an arm across Sam's shoulders. "Why did you pull Missy's hair?"

She felt the rise and fall of Sam's shoulders as he released a sigh. Missy sniffed.

"Sam?"

His voice came to her sounding small and scared. "I want my pa."

Alaina pulled the boy closer just as Missy burst into tears. The creak of the boards let her know Charlotte was coming to offer some assistance. They shared a look over the little girl's head. Alaina's mother touched Missy's shoulder. The child spun around and flung herself into Charlotte's arms, rocking the older woman off balance. Regaining her position, Charlotte pulled the child close and stroked her hair.

Alaina couldn't deny the children their need to see their father. If Jack showed up on the doorstep in the next few minutes, he could come along, but waiting for him, never knowing if he would forget or not, was not an option with Sam and Missy so obviously upset.

Alaina stood tall and stabbed a glance out the window. At least the rain had let up. She hated the idea of wading through the water standing in the streets from the constant downpours, but she had no choice. "Missy, Sam, let's get you bundled up and over to see your father."

Missy rubbed at her eyes and straightened in Charlotte's arms. "Really?"

Sam jumped to his feet. It was as if a great load had lifted from the boy's shoulders. "Will Jack come, too?"

"I don't know." Would this be what it was like to be married to Jack? He wouldn't come home to his family, always placing work above her? She might be able to endure the slights, as she had in the past, but for her to knowingly subject any children they might have together to the same thing seemed irresponsible. Or maybe she wasn't being fair to him. She hugged herself, not knowing what to think or feel. A shiver quaked through her.

"Alaina? Are you catching a chill?"

It had been easy to discount her mother's worries. Perhaps too easy. Her mother's expression was pinched with concern. For her.

"I'm fine, just. . ." She pressed her lips together as they began to form the words she knew would put sunshine on her mother's face. Words she was afraid to say because it meant part of a dream was dying. She drew in a slow breath. "When we get back, I'll help you with that dress. Then I'll cut out a new one—"

Her voice faltered the slightest bit. She braced herself mentally and met her mother's direct gaze. "Maybe I can have it done before I make the trip to Pittsburgh."

seventeen

Something sour churned Jack's gut at the dark windows and silence that met his many knocks on the door of Alaina's home. He feared Robert had already arrived to sweep Alaina away to some theater show and dinner, regaling her with stories of his new promotion and—

Jack heaved a sigh and shook his head. Alaina loved him. He loved her. Still, he had hoped to tell her the news himself, to wrest from her the promise that she would wait and to hear the words he so needed to believe—*I love you.*

Instead he turned and slogged his way back through the flooded streets. Water funneled and poured, his already wet shoes becoming saturated. He stopped long enough to stare up at the spire of the Presbyterian church, its stone face cold yet solid.

With nothing left to do but wander the streets, an idea that did not appeal to him in the least, Jack meandered back toward Cambria City. The evening stretched before him, long and dark. Robert's face, a smirk on his lips, loomed in Jack's mind. Taunting.

When he arrived at his house, he emptied the tin mug of its collection of water and set it back in place. At the small table, he glanced over the notes he'd made while writing his report on the dam and the theory he'd turned in to Fulton. They seemed nothing more than dry, cold facts. Sadness gripped Jack. For all the work he had put into his theory and the report on the dam, in trying to prove himself a good worker to Fulton, success meant nothing if he did not have Alaina by his side.

❧

To Alaina's way of thinking, Frank looked worse than the previous day. He appeared unfocused and acknowledged the children with wan joy. If Sam and Missy noticed their pa's decline, they didn't express their dismay.

Worry nibbled at the edges of Alaina's mind. What if Frank didn't live? She could hardly leave the children in an orphanage. Jack would know Frank's wishes and whether he had relatives or not, but gazing upon the sweet faces as they clung to their father's hands, she knew her own heart would struggle at the idea of saying good-bye.

"When are you coming home?" Missy asked.

Frank turned his head on the pillow, his face flushed.

Alaina worried the fever was ravaging his body faster than the wound.

"They had me up just before you got here, Missy. Wore me out. But I'm gettin' stronger."

His words brought a measure of relief. If he'd walked around, that explained his flushed face and the exhaustion. Alaina caught her mother's gesture and followed the flick of her hand that indicated a cane leaning against the wall. "What a beautiful cane, Frank. Did you make it?"

He blinked his eyes, and a slow smile curved his mouth. "One of the fellas carved it for himself when he got in an accident. He gave it to me yesterday before he left."

Missy grabbed up the cane and began to swing it around. Charlotte shook her head, and Missy set it back against the wall.

"You're feeling stronger then?" Alaina asked.

"Still have a bit of fever, but doctor says the wounds are healing well."

Missy resumed her post next to her father as he admonished them to be good and motioned the children, one by one, to lean in for a kiss.

Alaina made feeble attempts to converse with the children on the way home. Water in the streets made it necessary for her to carry Missy, while Sam clung to her mother's hand. The children appeared relieved by their visit and happier in spirit, splashing in puddles and laughing.

Though they grimaced at having to change out of their wet clothes, Alaina's promise of something hot to drink motivated them. Charlotte helped Sam peel off his sodden trousers as Alaina knelt to help Missy undress and pull a nightgown over her head, then ran a towel over her saturated locks to absorb excess water.

"Of all the times not to have hot cocoa," Charlotte fretted.

"Can I have tea?" Missy chirped. "And honey?"

Sam slipped onto the bench and swung his legs. Missy scampered over to her brother, damp hair already forming ringlets that framed her face.

Alaina pulled on the drenched fabric of her skirt to loosen her legs so she could stand. "I'll get the honey."

"Regular little angels." Charlotte smiled at the children. "You go change, Alaina. I'll get them their tea."

Grateful to be free of the saturated dress, Alaina pulled on a dry winter gown of worn brown wool to stave off further chill and hung her wet clothes over a metal tub to drip dry. She paused to stare out her window, unable to see much for the rain and darkening skies but well aware that her heart felt as dark and heavy as the fabric she'd just hung up. Having made the decision to sew a new dress locked her into going to Pittsburgh. Her mother would not let her back down from her promise now.

When she returned to the small kitchen, the first things she noticed were the drooping heads of both Sam and Missy.

She shared a smile with her mother, who mouthed, "*Bedtime.*"

Alaina pressed a hand against Missy's back. "Why don't I tuck you two in for the night?"

"Are you going to read us a story?" Missy asked.

"Not tonight. I don't think you could stay awake to hear it all."

Missy pooched her lip but said no more.

Sam slid off his chair and followed without protest. It took very little time to settle the two into the makeshift bed and say prayers. Missy dropped off sometime during Sam's prayer for their father and that the rains would stop, and then he stretched out beside his sister.

"I love you, Alaina," he said, his voice thick with exhaustion.

"I love you, too, Sam. Sleep well."

Missy stirred, sighed, and curled closer to her brother's side. Their heads were close together.

Alaina pulled the blanket up around their shoulders and cast another glance outside, her mind suddenly full of the many times she'd heard the rumor of the Lake Conemaugh Dam bursting open. Her mother never seemed bothered by the prospect, but Alaina knew if it did happen things would be bad for Johnstown. It nibbled at her that she couldn't leave her mother here, alone, with that threat looming large. Only the knowledge that her mother would discount the notion of the dam bursting flushed the idea from her mind.

She sighed. A dull headache gathered strength behind her eyes, and she rubbed the spot to ease the pressure.

"Alaina?" She turned to see the outline of her mother in the doorway. "There's got to be an inch of mud in the store, so I promised Mr. Heiser I'd clean it up this evening."

She nodded and swiped her hands down the skirt of her dress. "Why don't you let me do it?"

"If we work together, it'll go faster." Her mother's gaze slipped to the window behind Alaina. "Seems this rain will never stop."

"I was just thinking of that dam."

"It makes me glad we're not on the ground floor," Charlotte responded. She took a step closer to the doorway and paused. "Alaina, there's something I need to say to you."

The words glued Alaina to the spot. She braced for a verbal assault.

But her mother's expression softened. "I want you to understand why I'm so"—Charlotte squeezed her eyes shut—"so hard on you."

"You don't have to explain."

"I just don't want you to have to struggle. To have your heart broken by a man who can't keep his promises. Jack is so like your father."

"Why didn't you go West, too?" The question slipped out before Alaina gave it thought. In all the years since her father had left, she'd never ventured to ask, afraid of the response. She opened her mouth to apologize and take back the words.

Charlotte flinched but recovered quickly. Tears gathered in her eyes.

Alaina reached to offer some measure of comfort. When her mother turned and left the room, she followed, as if drawn by an invisible cord.

Her mother sat at the kitchen table and gestured for her to sit as well. "It's good that you ask, though the telling isn't easy." She pressed her lips together as great tears welled.

"Momma, you don't have—"

Charlotte gave her head a firm shake. "No. It's a question that needs answering. One that God has Himself been asking me. You see, your father did ask me." She clamped her hands together and squeezed her eyes shut. "I didn't want to go. It was hard for me to think of leaving Johnstown. He wouldn't budge either and told me he'd go ahead and send for us when he got settled."

"So he didn't abandon us?" Shock rolled over Alaina.

Her mother didn't respond for a long time as she sobbed into her hands.

The part of Alaina that wanted to comfort her mother dried up and blew away. Anger reared its ugly head. "How could you let me believe all these years that he left without ever looking back? He wanted us to go with him."

Charlotte nodded and smeared back the tears with the back of her hand. "I didn't realize you thought that. When he wrote letters, he never asked me again. I guess I took that as his way of saying he didn't want us."

That statement cut through Alaina's anger. She could understand her mother's reasoning. "Why did he stop writing?"

Charlotte shrugged. "I wish I knew. Between him not asking for us to join him and not writing, I've allowed myself to become"—she stared at the scarred tabletop—"bitter."

It made sense now. Her mother going back to church. The softening. Her reactions to Jack. Her bitterness. "But one thing you must understand, Momma, is that Jack is not Father. He wants to provide for me and make sure we're well taken care of."

"But that's no excuse for the way he forgets you."

Alaina nodded. "Yes, I know, but you've got to see him apart from Father. He's his own man."

Her mother stared at her for several minutes. "Yes, you're right. I've known that. Deep down inside, I've known that, but I still say you should be cautious. No man should treat you as Jack has." Charlotte reached out and laid a hand on Alaina's arm. "I have a surprise for you. I've been sewing dresses for you from scraps and leftover yardage my customers didn't care about."

"You have?"

"I saw the way you looked at him. At Jack. And I knew you would want to marry. I didn't want you to start out in rags. And I always hoped you might change your mind and go to college. To Pittsburgh. So I've got two dresses for you in my room."

Alaina understood the pleading in her mother's eyes and knew that she was being asked a question. She swallowed. "I'll try them on."

"Good, we can get you on the train west tomorrow morning." With that her mother left the room.

Alaina's head whirled with the generosity and suddenness of the gift, but something else, too—for the opportunity to see a side of her mother that she'd never seen before and for the knowledge that her father had not abandoned them. That was the most important of all the gifts she'd received.

eighteen

May 30, 1889

Jack breathed in the taste of freedom. Memorial Day meant a holiday. It meant festivities and banners and a nice tribute to the veterans of the Civil War. As he emerged from his shack and waved a hand at his landlady, who was busy herding her grandchildren indoors, he rubbed at the spot above his eyes where a dull ache had started to build after his restless night.

The fact that Robert had received *his* promotion burned in his mind. His anger flared and tasted hot on his tongue. After all he had done for Fulton, the man gave the position to Robert. Jack grunted and squeezed his eyes shut. Robert would continue to rub it in his face, he had no doubt, but he would have to take it. If he protested too loudly, Fulton just might fire him, and if he got fired, there would be no way he could ever afford to get married. Besides, he still had his plans.

Jack opened his eyes. Fulton's willingness to finance Jack's foray into inventing a better method of turning iron ore into steel still meant he had confidence in Jack's ability. And if the plans were accepted, it could mean a promotion to something far above Robert's new position. The very idea made Jack want to laugh. Oh, to see the expression on Robert's face then. And Alaina would be so proud of him.

In his mind, he could see the twinkle of pride in Alaina's dark eyes. He imagined her mane of hair, pulled back into ringlets, and her petite form gowned in the latest fashion. His heart pounded, and he lengthened his stride.

As he passed over the Little Conemaugh, he took note of the swollen, raging waters and how the water rose far above its normal level. He stabbed a glance at the pouting sky and made a mental note to take the train up to South Fork and check on the dam for himself.

Water stood knee-deep in some of the streets. He wondered what James Quinn of Foster and Quinn, a general store, thought of all the rain. He was one of the few citizens Jack knew who worried over the dam breaking.

"Hallo!"

Jack stopped in a deep puddle and waved as a hack pulled up beside him, the animal's back dark with water and sweat. "Ben, doing the business today, right?"

"Sure enough." Ben halted his horse right beside Jack. "The ladies especially aren't wanting to get their feet wet."

"I'd think on a day like this most would want to stay dry. The wet only adds to the chill in the bones."

"Ah, but there's something about Memorial Day that lightens the spirit." His grin turned knowing. "Steady stream heading to the depot. If you hop in, I'll get you there before she leaves."

Jack studied his friend's expression and wide grin and felt the first squeeze of dread. "Before she leaves?"

Ben's smile wilted. "Why, sure." The man glanced over Jack's shoulder and scratched his chin with the edge of the reins in his hands. "Took her, her momma, and the children over there for the ten fifteen to Pittsburgh. Want a ride?"

"Pittsburgh?" He tried to make sense of the news being dumped on him. Tried to understand why Alaina would be headed to Pittsburgh. Or maybe. . . "Her mother must be headed out to visit."

Ben raised his eyebrows. "From the chatter and the way she was dressed, Alaina's the one traveling."

Jack took a giant step forward and swung himself into the hack. "Hurry then." The jerk of forward motion slammed Jack against the seat. He closed his eyes, unable to understand Alaina's trip to Pittsburgh or her lack of communication on the matter. What about Sam and Missy? He dared not jump to conclusions without talking to her.

A church clock struck the hour of ten as the horse pulled up in front of the B&O station.

Jack pressed a coin into Ben's hand and spun toward the station. People lined the platform. A pile of trunks and boxes waited to be loaded.

He scanned the crowds until his eyes focused on two familiar faces. Sam and Missy each held one of Charlotte Morrison's hands. When Alaina's mother caught his gaze, her lips pressed together.

But the woman who stood up beside Missy, her back to him, hair pulled back in ringlets and wearing a gown of rich material cut in the latest style, was what set Jack's heart to beating. It was as if the mental image he'd had of her on his walk to Johnstown had materialized.

Alaina's mother nodded his direction.

Jack took a step closer.

Alaina turned, her eyes solemn, but the soberness faded into something else as he drew nearer.

He searched her face, the burgundy of her eyes, and tried to put meaning to the question he didn't know how to form.

"Jack." She lifted a hand and he caught it and brought it to his chest.

"Jack!" Missy's mouth curved into a smile.

He lifted his hand in a wave and forced a grin, all he could muster, then faced Alaina. "Ben told me you were here. Pittsburgh?"

"She's going to see the school like I've told her she should from the first," Charlotte offered.

Alaina turned. "Momma, please."

"Give my girl a chance. Some space. That's all I ask." Charlotte's no-nonsense tone held a note of desperation.

Jack felt dumbstruck by her words and the strange reality of Alaina's obvious decision to leave.

"The train is coming, Alaina," Charlotte murmured and shrank back with Sam and Missy. "Don't take long."

❧

She was a coward. She knew that now, facing Jack, seeing the anguish on his face.

Her mother had encouraged her to leave as soon as possible, and now she understood why. When she sat to write a letter to Jack, her mother insisted she hurry and pack. When she had paused from work with the intention of asking Victor Heiser if he'd carry the letter to Jack, Charlotte waved the idea away. "You've no time for that. He's had no time for you." And she'd allowed her mother to have sway over her.

But now, facing Jack, she knew she should have sought him out as her heart had told her to. "I've got to go, Jack. I've got to see what's out there for me."

"The college?"

"Momma has always wanted me to go. To see for myself. You know that."

"But what about us?"

Tears burned her eyes. Frustration mingled with love, but the frustration took firmer hold on her emotions. "Us?" She stared down at their joined hands and felt the well of all the forgotten plans and the excuses that followed. "I don't know. There never seemed to be any us. Just you and your determination to get rich. To invent whatever it is you—"

"Is it so wrong to want more for you than what you have now?"

It was the same old argument. She knew she would never get him to see that she needed *him* more than she needed *wealth*, and for the first time she recognized that she could not change him. She could not alter his drive. Only God could do that.

Her mother had been right all along. Marrying a man with such fierce focus meant she would be ignored. Was being ignored. In his bid to become rich, he'd become as fierce as his father, not in temper but in attitude.

The train came pounding into the station, leaving them suspended in pained silence as the vibration and noise drowned out any attempts at words.

His thumb stroked along the back of her hand. His tender touch impaled her heart and brought a wave of fresh tears to her eyes. He became a distorted image. When she raised her free hand to wipe the wetness from her cheeks, Jack produced a handkerchief in a swift motion.

The train settled into place, and people began to churn into action around them.

Alaina couldn't speak.

"Please don't leave," Jack whispered.

"I've got to do this." She wanted to say, "For me," but recognized how it seemed to reek of selfishness. Was she being selfish? Wasn't he? Marriage meant unselfish commitment. Not this. She had to release him.

"I lost the promotion. Is that why you're leaving?"

"No."

"You didn't know, then?"

Her lower lip trembled. "Robert told me."

"We'll make something work out."

"Why didn't you come over last night?"

"I did. You weren't home. I thought you might be out with Robert."

Stung by the veiled accusation, she caught her trembling lip between her teeth.

His free hand captured hers and he squeezed. "When you come back, we'll set a date. I can still work at Cambria, and if my plans go through. . ." The words tumbled from him like the raging waters of the Little Conemaugh. "Maybe we'll have enough money."

She shook her head, and his hands squeezed harder.

His eyes pleaded. "A trip away will help settle your mind. It'll be good for you to get away. They say distance makes love stronger."

"I can't—" Her voice caught on a sob. "Jack, please. Listen to me."

"The plans will work, and I'll have enough to marry you. We'll set the date for the end of June. If Fulton doesn't think the idea will take, then I'll work on another."

"Jack, listen!"

"All aboard!" the conductor called out.

"It's time, Alaina." Her mother hovered at her elbow like an anxious bird. "Your bag is aboard."

"Mother, please." Her tears fell freely now, and she faced Jack again.

His eyes held a wet sheen that beckoned her own tears.

Charlotte retreated as the conductor shouted out another call.

"I've tried, Jack." She licked her lips and tasted salt. "I've tried, but I can't do this. I can't marry you."

His chest rose sharply, and he pulled her into his arms, where the scent of his damp shirt filled her nostrils and made her close her eyes against the desire to take back what she'd just said.

"Alaina, don't leave me," he whispered in her ear. "Don't leave me."

"People are more important than things, Jack."

"You are important to me."

"When you think of me."

"But I do, Alaina. All the time. I do it for—"

She couldn't bear to hear him say it yet again. She wrenched herself from his grasp just as the conductor gave his last warning and the train whistle rent the air.

Jack reached to grab one of her hands, but she took a retreating step out of his reach. She took another step, shaking her head, unable to meet her mother's gaze, only able to see the rawness of emotion slashing sorrow into the angles of Jack's face.

She pressed a hand to her mouth and finally turned toward the train to run the final steps. The train started forward as she slid into her seat, alternately waving to her mother and grieving over the slumped shoulders and bowed head of the man she still loved. Her breath fogged the glass, and she resisted the urge to write the words "I'm so sorry, Jack" in the dew, but she felt them deep in her heart and soul.

nineteen

"You're a fool, Jack Kelly. A young, arrogant fool."

Jack sluiced a hand over his wet head and glared at his friend. "I came for some measure of comfort, and I get condemnation?"

Frank sat up in bed, propped by no fewer than four pillows, and pursed his lips. "Being near death helps give one new insight. You've treated that girl like a new hat. You don't give it the time of day unless it's a special holiday. Then you're glad to wear it."

He bit back the angry defense of his actions and said the words that had echoed through his mind ever since Alaina had disappeared onto the train. "I loved her."

He had wandered for hours, barely acknowledging the greetings from store owners and the barber. Not even the jokes about the high water or the sight of a man in a boat paddling down one road freed him from the chains of his remorse and grief. He loved her.

"Aye, boy-o, you loved her. As much as a pigheaded scrap of a man can love anyone."

His head snapped up. "You—"

Frank raised his hand and poked a finger into Jack's chest. Even from the hospital bed, Jack felt the sheer strength of the man in that one gesture. And something else. He saw the fury. "Wake up! How many times did you promise her you'd see her and not show up?"

Jack firmed his jaw. "She knew I had to work on my plans and—"

"How long you been feeding yourself that line, boy? How long you been ignoring what's important? Where's your faith, man? God Himself tells us to love a woman more than we love ourselves."

"I know that verse. It's for the married."

"And you were planning on treating her good only then?"

"You know what I mean."

Frank rose up. "It doesn't matter now, does it? You ignored her in favor of gain, and now you've lost everything."

With great effort, Jack stamped back the tirade of words that perched on his tongue.

Frank must have seen his struggle, only he didn't hold back. "Your money will keep you warm. But will it give you the companionship and love that a woman can give? Wake *up*, Jack!"

"I can see"—he sucked in a ragged breath—"that I made a mistake seeking you out. I thought you might help bolster a fella in his time of need."

"You thought I'd give you sympathy and soothe your pride. Pride isn't meant to be soothed, boy. It's meant to be repented of."

"I grew up poor, Frank. Remember? No one could ever be more humbled by that than me."

"It's become a pride to you to gain riches and overcome your past. You want what you didn't think you had as a boy and what you now think is owed you." Frank rubbed the back of his neck, and Jack caught the wince of pain that the simple movement caused him. "How many times has Alaina told you she doesn't need to be the wife of a rich man?"

Jack froze. Had he talked to Alaina? He ran his fingers along the rim of his damp hat, regarding the roughness of the material.

Alaina's face filled his mind. Her pleading words echoed to him. *"I don't need to be rich, Jack."* He pounded his hat back on his head and spun. "I'll leave you to your own company then."

"Jack."

He spun around as Frank relaxed back, deep into the pillows, and closed his eyes. "Do us all a favor and keep your eye on that dam. Heard there's more rain on the way. That thing's not going to hold forever."

❧

As the train picked up speed, Alaina struggled against the burn in her throat and the even worse hole where her heart had been. She rested her forehead against the window and prayed for strength and wisdom. . .and Jack. Always for Jack.

Releasing him had been the hardest thing. On so many levels she knew it was the answer, the right thing to do, but the pain consumed her like fire.

The conductor asked for her ticket just as the tears began staining her cheeks all over again. His kindly face smiled down at her. "If there's anything you need, ma'am. . ."

"Thank you," she croaked out, but the show of sympathy unraveled what little composure she'd managed to hold on to. Turning back to the window, she buried her face in her hands and let loose the torrent in a series of soft sobs that made her grateful the train didn't travel with a full car of passengers.

She seemed to move in a haze, partially aware of her mother's sister meeting her and the ride to the small, but richly furnished home. Her aunt's stream of chatter, so contrary to her mother's quiet nature, relieved her of the need to keep a constant dialogue going, and though sunshine spilled down in Pittsburgh, Alaina felt grateful for the warmth of the new, heavy dress material.

When her Aunt Joanne, or Aunt Jo as she preferred, took her on a hackney ride up Eighth Street to the college, the immenseness of the building overwhelmed her senses.

"I'm so excited to have you move here and attend," her aunt chattered on. "You've kept up your studies? Knowing your mother, I'm sure you have." The older woman twisted on her seat and shaded her eyes to squint at the building. A deep sigh escaped her. "Oh, how lovely. Brings a thrill to my heart every time I think of women in higher education. We'll give those men something to think about, right, dear?"

Her aunt seldom required a response, and Alaina allowed her to continue the one-sided conversation. She needed to say something. Wanted to say quite a lot, really, but not about college or Latin or anything else related to life outside of Johnstown. It felt too much like acknowledging a life without Jack.

Oh, God, what have I done? Am I in Your will now, here, or in Johnstown?

twenty

The long ride up from Johnstown had accomplished a diversion, though he couldn't remember what he'd been thinking about or getting on and off the train. He recalled the crash of the raging Little Conemaugh River that followed the trail fourteen miles up from Johnstown to the South Fork Fishing and Hunting Club. When he disembarked in South Fork and found a horse, he rode straight up to the dam.

Frank's words had spooked him. All the talk of the dam breaking. Yet it looked firm and solid and unyielding to him as he sat astride the horse. He spent an hour riding by the spillway stream and remembering the picnic he and Alaina had taken beside the beautiful fall of water. And at the crest of the dam, where the water lay a mere four feet from the top, he recalled the proposal. The sun in her hair. The smile that lifted his spirits and set his heart into a gallop.

Every memory they'd shared seemed to rip at him until he felt heavy and realized the light was fading from the sky. He finally kicked the horse into a gallop and took the short trip back down to South Fork.

There he had the horse looked after and crossed to a small restaurant, where he ordered the special and listened to the people talk about the rain. As he speared a chunk of roast and lifted it to his lips, he knew he needed rest and wondered if he would be able to sleep at all. He stared down at his nearly full plate and felt the food he had eaten ball up in his stomach. He pushed the plate away and scrubbed a hand over his hair and down his neck.

An older man entered the restaurant and, seeing the vacant chair across from Jack, headed straight for it. Tom Hennesey was a talker who often hauled club members up to the lake, including Alaina, which was how they'd come to know each other. Jack inclined his head as the man straddled the chair, then laid a hand on the seat and pulled it closer to the table. "Hear Johnstown's a swimming hole."

Jack couldn't help but grin at the man's choice of words. "Saw a rowboat going down a street on the west side."

Tom spit out a laugh. "You'd think old Johnstown would learn a thing or two 'bout being in a floodplain. Guess they liken themselves as ducks. Me, I'm getting myself to higher ground. If any more rain's a-coming, you won't see me swimming for my life. Nope. I'll be standing atop the mountain laughing."

"You think it's going to break?"

"You know these mountains, son. Thunder gusts happen all the time. And this weather"—he scratched at his chest—"been all over the place this month. Makes my bones weary and worries my mind something fierce."

Jack pushed his plate in the man's direction. "I'm done if you want to finish off what's there."

Tom guffawed, one gnarled hand clamping the edge of the dish and pulling it his way. "Don't mind if I do. Shame to see good food go to waste." His eyes traced over Jack's face from beneath bushy brows. "You so lovesick you can't eat? Heading up to see your girl?"

A knot swelled in Jack's throat. "She's not up there. Her family pulled out early."

"Seems strange. What you doing up here then?"

Jack's conscience pulled at him. His tongue held the explanation as if the saying of it would somehow dispel his sense of unreality. After all, Alaina could change her mind. He really had meant that the time away would be good for her. For them. But despite his conviction, the thought did little to ease the pain.

Tom stopped chewing and craned his neck, eyes more alert than Jack wanted. Jack scraped his chair back just as Tom handed down his verdict. "You got yourself girl trouble."

Jack tried to shake off the comment.

But Tom waved him to stay put. "Got a thing or two to tell you about women. Now don't look that way. I ain't spilling anything I shouldn't be. Was married myself once. She died a few years back of the diptheria that swept through here in '79. You'd've been too young to remember much of it. Lot of children died, but got me real shook when my wife came down sick." Tom's brows beetled, and he tore off a corner of a biscuit and sopped up the juice from the roast before popping it into his mouth. "She was my life."

Jack edged his seat closer. "You mean your wife?"

"Nope. Said it just like I meant it. She was my life. Took real good care of each other. When she died, I thought I'd 'bout near shrivel up and blow away." Tom paused long enough to tear off another piece of biscuit.

"Why are you telling me this?"

Tom's head snapped up. "So's you can make good and sure to listen to what it is she's trying to tell you."

"Trying to tell me. . .?"

"Woman doesn't free a man up unless she's got rock-solid good reason. I've met your girl. She's a good one. Good heart. Gentle. Not hard to see that, even for an old one like me. Reminded me of my Rebecca. That's the kind of woman a man needs most." Tom paused. It seemed the man was working up to something else.

Already Jack had been surprised by the man's talk. Most men joked and lamented being married, especially as the family grew. One of the reasons Jack wanted so much to be free from poverty before marrying. So many men had struggled to put food on the table, working twelve-hour shifts, six days a week. It wearied him to think of struggling like that the rest of his life.

"What about the kind of man a woman wants?" The words slipped out. Embarrassed by the question, Jack moved to rise.

"Reckon a woman's wants aren't so much different from a man's. Someone to share life with. To love on and be loved by. All the other stuff is just leaves on the tree."

Pain swelled in Jack's heart as he stared down at the man and allowed the words to sink in. They chipped at him. Could it be that his need to make a comfortable living was more for him than Alaina? She'd told him so often enough. He wondered how it would feel to live with her as husband and wife and struggle as the other men struggled. Jack swiped a hand over his damp hair. "I need to go."

"Go?" Tom chuckled. "Where you planning on going this time of night? You needing a place to stay, I reckon you can bunk at my place."

⁂

Dear Jack. . .

Those were the only words Alaina had managed to write in the hour since she'd retired to her room. She had escaped after convincing her Aunt Jo that her quietness stemmed from nothing more than exhaustion. Truer words she would never speak.

She cradled her head in the palm of her hand and stared at the paper and those two words. Tomorrow she would begin a tour of the college and look into requirements and tuition needs.

Her aunt had promised, many times, to help along those lines. "Regis left me quite comfortable, and I made a vow to your mother that I would help if you chose to attend. Your being here would be company for me, too. You might even meet some nice young man during your time here."

If she had suspected her mother and her aunt had been in close communication, that statement assured her of it. She could just imagine her mother's long dissertation to her aunt about Jack's perceived inadequacies.

Alaina squeezed her eyes shut. *I don't want to be here, God. I want to be back in Johnstown. With Jack.*

But she knew Jack needed to see her in a different light. Breaking the engagement had been the right thing to do. She felt it deep in her spirit, even if the shadow in Jack's blue eyes drained her of joy.

How can I cause such hurt yet know I'm right in my decision?

The question brought the story of Christ to her mind. And Abraham and Isaac. Also, the widow who sacrificed not just her life but the life of her only son for a man she didn't know. Of God's sacrifice in watching His only Son suffer and die. Such pain. Beauty for ashes.

Instead of continuing the letter, she slipped the sheet of paper from the surface and crumpled it into a tight ball as a tear splashed onto the surface of the small writing desk.

twenty-one

May 31, 1889

Jack woke with a rush of anxiousness that left him with a dull headache. A form moved through the shadows. Disoriented, he sprang to his feet.

He heard the strike of a match, and a sudden flare of light brought Tom's face into clear view.

Jack relaxed.

"You hear that?" Tom asked.

That's when he understood why he'd awoken so quickly. "Rain."

"That's not rain, son. That's the worst mess of water rushing down from the sky that I've ever heard. We just might find ourselves riding down this mountain on a mud slide." Tom brought the lantern to the table close to the one small window on the front of his house.

Jack narrowed his eyes to see outside, but nothing except the glint of light off a sheet of water met his vision. The deluge sounded like a live thing trying to crush the house flat. "We should check on things," Jack spat. "Make sure everyone is safe."

Tom considered a moment and then shook his head. "It's eleven thirty. Decent folk are sound asleep. This might not last long anyhow. You know how quick the storms can be through here." He lifted the chimney and blew out the light. "Best get some rest. Tomorrow might be a long day."

Jack lay back down on the hard floor and pulled the thin blanket over his shoulders. Sleep wouldn't come. Instead, his mind labored under the idea of what it would be like to lose Alaina. She might never return. The idea left him hollow and scared, and for the first time, Jack knew no amount of money was worth being alone.

Through the night he lay awake reviewing the string of events, missed dates, broken promises, and Alaina's adamant, "I don't need to be rich," over and over. And every moment was underscored by Frank's observations of his selfishness and pride. His friend's words bruised him.

He swallowed and rolled to his side, then punched at the rolled-up blanket he used as a pillow. The threadbare blanket encompassed everything he felt about being poor. It made him feel fragile and weak. Vulnerable.

A picture of her smiling face flashed into his mind and froze there. *Alaina*. She would laugh at the prospect of threadbare blankets and a leaky roof. It would become an adventure for her to figure out a way to make things better. Even the small apartment she shared with her mother lacked the dreariness he would expect from someone poor. Perhaps because Alaina and Charlotte took time to make it look cozy and warm.

Jack rolled to his back and blinked up at the thin ceiling, where the sound of rain had grown more vicious. Alaina radiated a peace and contentment he didn't have. It drew him to her and was one of the reasons he felt it so easy to break promises. He knew she would always be there. Loving. Kind. Content.

Well, she's not here now, Jack, old boy.

While her faith had grown, his had shrunk. Frank was right, though it pained him to admit it. He'd become selfish. In his pursuit of what he wanted, what he thought was best for *them*, he'd tuned out Alaina.

A tug at his conscience shed light on his cluttered thoughts. He'd tuned out God as well. The balancing factor in his life. The One who never failed to show him how to love others first and himself last had faded into the background along with Alaina. No—he squeezed his eyes shut—no, he had shoved them into the background, rejecting them because he thought accepting them meant he would be forced to accept being poor. And humble. And vulnerable.

And because he'd been unable to forgive his father.

"People are more important than things."

Could he forgive his father his weaknesses? Or would he allow his private bitterness against Don Kelly to destroy him? How could he forgive?

The dark night so many days ago when he'd agonized over his plans and Pastor's sermon, he recalled asking the same question. How could he choose to forgive? Except now he knew the answer. It was simply that: a choice.

He closed his eyes. It would not be easy, but it would be a start.

God, I've been so full of myself, the prayer began, as he drew in a ragged breath and exhaled his confession. *So full of myself and so scared. . .*

ॐ

"Get up! We gotta get out of here."

Jack bolted upright at Tom's frantic voice. He stared out the window into gray light. Jack rubbed at his right temple, where a dull ache reminded him of his rough night, but the memory also brought something else, a peace that he hadn't felt in a long time. "What's going on? Is it still raining?"

Tom didn't answer but jabbed a finger at a skillet with a lone pancake. "Grab it and let's go. I wanna know about that dam. Water's running high all up and down South Fork. It must be at the crest of that dam, and I don't want to be anywhere near here when it goes."

"I'll get the horses."

"Already got them. Was out this morning and down to Stineman's supply." Tom finally turned, his eyes tripping over Jack's face. "They was saying how everything was fine. That the dam was going to hold."

"Who?"

"Boyer and the fella from the club. Beedwell, I think his name was."

"You don't believe them?"

"All's I'm saying is, this weather isn't helping. Look at the Little Conemaugh. It's a raging beast." Tom paused and pressed his lips together. "I've seen a lot of things that are unnatural, and I'm not much of a praying man, but I pray God have mercy on me today because if that dam goes. . ."

Tom dashed outside as Jack pulled on his shirt and leapt to follow before Tom left him behind. Their horses splashed up Railroad Street, where a small crowd clustered in front of George Stineman's general store.

"That's that Parke fella," Jack heard Tom mumble. "If he's here, things must be bad."

Before he could ask who the "Parke" fella was, Tom kicked his horse and took off up Lake Street toward the dam. Jack matched the pace but eased his horse some when he saw just how badly the road to South Fork had deteriorated because of the rain.

The road forked, and Tom swerved to the right where the trees parted. When the old man pulled his horse up tight, the animal almost sat down in the road. Jack came abreast of the slack-jawed man. He snapped his head to follow Tom's line of vision and felt dread shoot down his spine. A bunch of men, looking small from the distance, raced along the breast of the dam, seemingly at the command of a man on horseback.

"They're trying to raise the height of the dam." Tom's words came hard and fast. "There's no way they'll have time. No way."

Jack didn't wait to hear more. He nudged his horse hard toward the breast of the dam, shocked when he saw that the water was nearly level with the road.

Tom came up beside him and reached out his hand to grab the bridle of Jack's horse. "Don't go out there. It's too dangerous."

✺

"Your heart isn't here, is it, dear?"

Alaina realized she'd been staring at the food on her plate, lulled into silence by her aunt's continuous chatter. "I'm sorry,

Auntie. I guess I'm not that hungry after all."

"I expect this has to do with that boy your mother is so desperate to get you away from."

Alaina gasped. "She told you about Jack?"

"Of course. Charlotte tells me a great many of her fears. It's what sisters do, you know. Oh, for a while she never told me anything, mostly when I was married to Regis, but I believe that was because she was embarrassed. She felt that I was far above her socially. How absurd is that? It's not as if I'm better than her at all. She's my sister and I love her, but she loved your father. His silence has hurt her very badly."

Alaina opened her mouth but could think of nothing to say.

"Your mother simply doesn't want to see you hurt like she was hurt."

"Yes, I know. She told me about refusing to go West. Why didn't she go, Auntie?"

"Why, indeed. She's stubborn. Would rather nurse her wound to him than acknowledge the wound she inflicted." Her aunt shoved her plate back. "Now I want to hear about this Jack fellow from you."

"I—" Alaina gulped and locked her hands together under the table. "Jack wants what's best for us." She expected her aunt to charge into the conversation to dispute that, but she remained silent. "He works for Cambria Iron but has a great mind for inventing. He keeps trying to come up with a better way to make iron into steel, but his ideas haven't worked so far."

Her aunt nodded. "He is a decent sort?"

"He's a very hard worker."

"Alaina"—her aunt's gaze became direct—"why do I sense a hesitancy in you regarding this young man?"

The young maid appeared to refill Alaina's juice glass. She crossed to fill Aunt Jo's glass as well.

"Thank you, Tia," Aunt Jo said.

"My pleasure, ma'am."

Aunt Jo sipped her juice and relaxed back in her chair. "I

fear being alone has relaxed my manners. I'm not nearly so strict as other ladies, but then I don't really care to be." She gave the young maid a kind smile that Tia returned before disappearing. "She wants to go to the college."

Alaina tilted her head. "Tia?"

"Yes." She lowered her voice. "I agreed to pay her twice what other maids earn if she would promise to save half for the first year of tuition."

Warmth for her aunt's kindness flooded through Alaina. How different her mother seemed from her Aunt Jo. But the thought shamed her when she remembered her mother's surprise and fingered the excellent material of her stylish new dress.

"Now, your young man. Your mother seems to worry ever so much about your marrying him. Too much, in my mind, but then I never had children to worry and fret over, so I'm sure I don't understand."

Alaina ordered her thoughts before she spoke, relieved when her aunt didn't press her to hurry or distract her with more questions. She took a bite of the now-cold pancakes and a long swallow of the orange juice. "Jack is handsome and fun." Her heart swelled at the thought of his antics, and she pressed the napkin to her lips to cover the smile.

"No need to go all prim and proper. I've been in love, too, and well know the giggling foolery of a smitten woman. Regis was a trickster, he was, and he made me laugh on many occasions when I would have cried. That is a priceless attribute."

"Yes." Alaina nodded. "He loves children and. . .and. . ." Words suddenly failed her, and she stared down at the congealed food on her plate.

"Then why are you here?"

Aunt Jo's soft question beckoned forth the only answer Alaina could give. "Because Momma wanted me to come so badly."

"My sister is blind to your needs. In her effort to protect you, she is unable to see your love for this young man."

"There is more to it, though, Aunt Jo. Sometimes Jack. . . forgets me."

"Excuse me?"

Alaina put some steel in her voice. "I said, sometimes he forgets me."

"I thought that's what I heard you say. But please, forgets you how?"

She explained about the missed dates and watched her aunt's expression for signs of disgust or outrage, as she often saw on her mother's face.

"It seems to me you have a young man who is hardworking and diligent. Not bad traits at all. But"—Aunt Jo let the silence grow—"I think there are some things he needs to realize. To start off, he needs to see what a treasure he has in you, that it's not in the hope of getting rich."

"How will he see that?"

Aunt Jo's smile grew slowly. "That, my dear, is something the Good Lord will have to impress upon him. If the two of you are meant to be together, then nothing can separate you."

twenty-two

Jack heaved the pickax. His muscles bunched as he pulled it to his shoulder and swung downward again with every bit of strength he could muster. The tight group of men around him worked like a machine, each man's cuts with pickax or shovel in perfect synchronization with the next man's. But Jack knew, even as his swing came down seconds before that of the man across from him, that it would never work.

"It's no use. We can't cut through," someone shouted through the rain.

Jack's hands slipped on the wet handle, and he adjusted his grip before raising the tool for another plunge into the rocky slope. He flipped the pickax to the side with the point midswing, but even the point did little more than make an inch-deep indentation.

"Clear out! Clear out! It's going over." The tight ball of men working on carving out another spillway to relieve the pressure of the water building behind the dam scattered.

Jack raised his head to see a sheen of water eat away at the dirt and rock that had been thrown up in the middle of the dam to increase its height.

"Jack!" Tom yanked on his sleeve and got him moving. When the two men stopped on the far end of the dam, the water had begun the slide over the top and dropped in a silvery sheet. "It's soaked through and won't hold much longer," Tom hollered.

Jack jerked. "Warn them!"

Tom's hand held him firm. "It's been done. The line from here isn't working yet. They sent someone down to South Fork."

Jack's mind churned. "I need to get to Johnstown."

Tom faced him, the man's hands clenching his shoulders with a strength Jack would have never guessed him to possess. "Word is, roads are washed out. If you go out now, you could get caught in it."

Even as Tom's words penetrated, the water sluicing over the dam grew in volume, like an insatiable beast that had tasted the sweetness of liberty and wanted more.

"I've got to go."

Tom shook his head. "It's no use. They sent another boy down to South Fork just minutes ago and another man went to clear his family out. I let them have our horses."

Tension grew in Jack's stomach, clenching it hard and churning the cold pancake he'd eaten into acid.

❧

"It seems to me you were rushed to get out of there. He is no doubt devastated and confused, perhaps even angry."

Alaina stared out the window at the street and recognized the train depot. "Auntie, I thought we were headed back to the college."

Aunt Jo's eyes twinkled. "So *you* thought. *If I were Alaina*, I thought to myself, *I'd want to head back to Johnstown as soon as possible and talk to my young man.*"

"But if I leave, Momma will be so unhappy."

Aunt Jo's chin tilted to a stubborn angle. "Leave Charlotte to me." The carriage pulled up in front of the station, and her aunt waited for the driver to offer his hand before descending. "Have your say with Jack and bring him and your mother with you back here." Her eyes sparkled. "That will give me a chance to help your mother see reason. Maybe she'll even swallow her stubborn pride and move back here to live with me like I've offered a thousand times."

Excitement and nervousness clawed at Alaina as she crossed the station and perused the length of the train.

"Looks like Mr. Pitcairn is traveling today." Aunt Jo's long finger pointed. "That's his private car right there. Oh, but they're calling for boarding. Have a nice trip and come back whether Jack sees the light or not. Pittsburgh has some quite handsome single young men."

Alaina waved to her aunt until the woman faded to a speck and the train's momentum made looking back a stomach-churning experience. Ash from the engine flew through the window and smeared on Alaina's dress when she brushed at it. She pushed the window up and settled in to work out what she would say, both to her mother and to Jack.

Jack.

An urgency to pray gripped her. Pray for whom? For Jack? Her heartbeat picked up speed, and she bowed her head and closed her eyes, but her mind blanked. *Lord?* Her mind filled with the view of the valley from the Lake Conemaugh Dam. *Lord, have mercy. I don't know what this means, but protect Momma and Jack, Frank and—*

A raindrop splashed through an open window onto her hand, and Alaina wiped it away as a sickening dread filled her. Rain. The dam. All the rumors of the dam breaking and the water sweeping through the valley. Dread choked her throat. She prayed fervently for what seemed like hours and then raised her head to see the landscape blurred by gray rain. In places she glimpsed the high water pooling in lowlands. And all the time, she breathed the same prayer, the urgency not lessening, but her own fear growing until the tension in her body churned an ache in her head.

twenty-three

Jack kept the horse at a gallop as much as possible during the fourteen-mile ride down to Johnstown from South Fork. The animal he'd borrowed in South Fork seemed game for the journey and displayed fine spirit despite the drizzle, raging water, and washed-out roads.

At places along the route, Jack had to stop and pick his way over a washout, but the horse never hesitated when Jack dug his heels deep in the animal's sides. Just as the valley came into view and the terrain flattened, the horse's strides became more sure, but a deep-throated rumble brought Jack's attention around. He spurred the animal, sure he knew what danger caused the sound. The water would have cut through by now.

Jack crossed the bridge into Johnstown when another rumble swelled through the air. He dared a glance over his left shoulder and saw a black mist and a yellow wall of water. His heart jumped and pounded. Cold sweat popped up along his back and forehead. He pulled the horse up hard and vaulted to the ground. Turning, he gave the animal a hard smack on the rump, and it took off.

Jack flung open the door of a tall building and raced up the steps. His mind absorbed details as he went. The banister and rails, the doors with numbers lining the hall. A hotel. As he raced up the second flight of steps, he heard voices, frantic and high-pitched, underscored by the deeper tones of a man's voice. And over that a deep rumbling that built into a deafening roar. A gust of wind sucked up the steps. Jack's legs burned.

On the third-floor landing, he saw a man at the window and a huddle of people crouching in a corner. Shadows held the people captive, but the deafening roar, growing louder by the second, had etched lines of terror in their faces.

"Is there an attic?" he yelled above the roar.

The man at the window ran toward them, arms waving. "Get up the steps. All the way up!"

As one, the group rose. Jack's eyes darted around the room, but he saw no stairway until the man flung open a narrow door to reveal an equally narrow flight of steps. The house shuddered hard. Water shot through the glass of the windows, sending shards across the room as water poured through the new opening. Beneath their feet, the floor rose like a raft, carrying them to the ceiling. Jack crouched and lay flat to avoid becoming crushed against the ceiling. He rolled over, and the floor disintegrated beneath him. Screams and shouts rent the air around him as people were set adrift in the raging, swirling waters.

Jack struck out. He gasped at the cold water, spat at the wetness invading his nostrils and pushing into his mouth. More cries and screams came to his ears, moans, all sifted through the roar and crash of water, the tearing of wood and rip of nails popping. Lifting and tumbling, the water swelled and churned until the building itself simply disappeared. Jack fought the pull of the undercurrent, shocked to see the menacing pewter of the sky.

A hard shove brought pain to his shoulder. Water filled his ears, and something grabbed his leg. A hand? He bent in two to feel for whatever it might be, but the grip released. A huge piece of debris barreled toward him, a man and woman huddled together. Jack saw the woman's mouth open. . .then she was gone. The water rolled him. When he braced his body, he sank lower, so he relaxed, exhausted. His hand touched something hard, and he squeezed his eyes shut to clear water. A board floated away and then shot back toward him, taunting him with its nearness.

He moved that direction, arms leaden, legs limp. Every movement brought him closer to the board. The board shifted direction and flowed away as if sucked by a gaping mouth toward a distant point. With the last bit of strength he could muster, he made a grab for the piece of wood as it began to twist away again. Jagged pain raced up his arms as his hands slid over the rough wood and he pulled himself partially onto the surface.

Jack's nerves burned. He floated, pulled by the current. Afraid to raise his head and see more terrible sights, he knew the sounds were enough.

When he'd rested and his vision cleared, he lifted his head to take in his surroundings. Rooftops. Boards. A dead horse. As he watched, a tall building, of which only the top floor was visible, swayed and plunged beneath the surface. He began to paddle toward the distant mountain.

"People are more important than things." Through a fog of exhausted uncaring, he saw Alaina's smile. The smile dimmed into a frown and her arms stretched out. *"You can do it, Jack."*

The icy water began to work its brand of paralysis. Moving became more difficult. Jack clung to the words he heard in his mind, Alaina's image having long faded. Something moved around his legs. Water began to swirl around his body and pull at him. He tightened his hold on the board.

Oh, God, was all he had time for before another wave engulfed him.

❧

"What is it? Why have we stopped?" Alaina put the questions to the conductor.

"Everything is fine, I'm sure, miss. We'll move along shortly."

Left with little to do but wait, Alaina watched the muddy, swollen river rush by not far from where they sat.

A woman farther up in the car gasped, and the man behind her shot from his seat and pushed his face against the window. His expletive accompanied a man surging into view on the swift river, clinging to a board. More debris swirled and tossed in the angry waters, and another person shot by.

Everyone on the train seemed frozen to the spot. Then the men in Alaina's car seemed to come alive all at once. More exclamations, more shuffling of feet, then they started getting off, one by one. The women hovered at the windows and watched in terror as a house crashed into a clot of debris.

Within minutes the men had found makeshift poles or anchored each other in an effort to catch people. A young man cinched a cord around his waist and struck out toward the house caught in the trees. Alaina watched the man's struggle with bated breath. He twisted and turned every which way, at last arriving at the shattered house. When he emerged, he held something close.

"He's got a baby!" one of the women next to Alaina exclaimed.

"Where is this coming from?" A woman threw the question out to no one in particular.

Alaina collected the words, then spoke them out loud, her lips dry and her eyes burning. "Johnstown. It's from Johnstown. The dam must have broken."

"True. There's too much water for it to be a simple flood," someone else replied.

"Do you know someone from there?" a dark-haired woman asked the question of Alaina.

"My mother and fian—" Her voice broke. "Fiancé are there."

"Oh, how terrible for you."

Genuine sympathy oozed from the woman and broke down every ounce of Alaina's composure. Her legs became weak, and she folded herself onto the seat, buried her face, and allowed the sobs she'd held back to break free. Jack's expression at the train station filled her mind and made her despair that much harder to bear.

Momma. Jack. Missy and Sam.

The list of names marched across her mind and further deepened the well of her cries. She felt the pressure of two arms cradle her close and cared not who it was who offered the comfort. She clung to the person as if she herself had been set adrift in the wildly raging river.

"Look!" she heard one of the women say.

The person holding her tensed, and Alaina could feel her

benefactor's body shift position, though her arms remained around her. Alaina kept her eyes closed.

"He's going back."

"No!"

Alaina raised her head then, and the raven-haired woman smiled down at her and stroked her cheek. Then she, too, rose and crossed to the windows.

"He is going back."

"One of us should tend that baby."

"There's a new mother in the next car. Perhaps she could care for the wee one."

The conversation between the women swirled around Alaina. She felt detached and afraid. A deep coldness clenched down on her spine and made her shiver, and still they talked.

"He's bringing out someone else."

"He must be exhausted."

"Oh, the child won't be all alone then. Thank the Good Lord."

She never understood where the strength to rise came from or what drew her to the window, but when she saw the rescued woman come closer, carried by one of the men, her dress little more than rags around her, Alaina felt the shock shedding from her mind and body. She took a step back as the man carrying the woman answered the frantic waving of her fellow passengers and brought the rescued woman on board. She sucked in a breath and went to the place where the man settled the shivering, wet form onto a seat. "Mrs. Newton!" Alaina knelt, her skirts billowing around her.

The woman's gaze landed on her, dull and unfocused.

"You know her. That's good. Keep talking to her while we get her warm." Alaina's benevolent companion turned away and raised her voice to be heard. "I need any spare clothing you can offer. Hurry now! Someone run over and check on the babe. The news will help her."

Alaina remained where she was and took the cold, pale hand in her own. "I'm the daughter of your dressmaker, Mrs.

Newton. I remember you well. My mother worked from Heiser's store."

Mrs. Newton's pale eyes ran over Alaina's face. She blinked slowly, and a shiver shook her slender form. "It's all gone," she whispered.

Alaina strained to hear the words and swallowed as comprehension dawned. *All gone?* She pressed the back of her hand to her mouth and gulped. *All. Gone. Momma? Jack?*

She never knew if she fell back or was pushed aside as the women began to bundle the woman in the spare clothing, but as Alaina regained her balance and rose to her feet, she knew she could not stay, stranded in Sang Hollow, four miles from Johnstown. Determination stiffened her spine, and she slipped off the car and into the rain.

twenty-four

Jack clung to the board, wrapping his arms around it to give his muscles some relief. He wanted to crawl on top of it, but his strength vanished. Blood trickled down his neck, and he dared not touch the spot where the water had slammed him into the brick wall of a building.

A hoarse scream for help, a man's voice, came quietly and then more loudly as Jack's raft floated closer to a home, only the attic visible and the lone man on top. With what little strength he could muster, he paddled closer. The current tried to drag him back, but he kept on. One hand. Then the other. One leg. Then the other. The man quieted as Jack drew closer.

"Jump!" Jack screamed. "Jump, and I'll come to you."

The man twisted on the rooftop, back and forth, as if he searched for some other means of escape. In the dim light, Jack felt the familiarity of that profile, of that form. He dug deep into the violent gray waters to push himself closer to the distraught man.

"Help me!"

"Here!" Jack yelled. The man's eyes landed on Jack. A jolt of surprise ripped through him. *Robert.*

"You going to save me, Kelly?" The question was both wistful and arrogant.

A quiver vibrated through the water, and Jack saw the house shift ever so slightly. "You've got to get off there. Now. Jump before it goes under."

Robert scrambled closer. "Playing the hero?"

The waters shifted direction again. Jack's struggle to get closer to the house morphed into an all-out fight to keep from being crushed against it. He threw out one hand to brace himself even as he fought to retain his grip on the board. Too late, the water jerked the wood from his grasp. He lunged and caught it, just as the water drove him back and slammed his head against the corner of the brick. He heard a scream but didn't know if it was from his own lips or not. Pain slid up his neck, and his vision dimmed.

When his sight cleared, he lessened his grip and felt the water begin to tear at him again, this time in the opposite direction. He tightened his hug on the board and squinted up at the roof, trying to make sense of things. Warmth on his neck let him know the extent of his injury.

Cool water surged upward and engulfed his body. Jack struggled to hold his place close to the roof, to think what had brought him here.

"People. . .more important. . .than things." Alaina's voice.

The words stoked his mind, and the mist over his thinking rolled back. The cry came again, like that of a hurt animal. Close. He looked up and blinked, trying to focus. Robert's form became clear, and Jack's mind flooded with what had become his mission. He sucked air into his lungs and tried to pull strength from somewhere deep inside him.

No. He didn't have to do this. Robert's weight on the board could sink them both. No one would blame him. No one would know.

Air flowed around him, and he blinked slowly. Robert stood for all he had wanted and lost, and the man had rubbed his victory in Jack's face.

Did it mean anything now? Could he doom the man to death without trying to save his life?

God, help me.

He lifted his head. "Robert." No. His voice didn't carry over the noise of the water, of distant screams and crashing. Of Robert's own panicked cries. Jack swallowed and raised his head higher. "Robert! Robert, I can't stay here. The building's going to go. Jump!"

Robert stilled. His head tilted as if he heard something Jack did not.

Like an invisible hand, Jack felt a shove that sent him surging backward, away from the rooftop. Even as the distance between them grew, Jack saw the building sway. Desperate, he tried one more time. "Robert, jump!"

Another shift of the house seemed to jerk Robert back to reality. He ran up the roof, slipped, caught himself, and began a desperate crawl to the ridge.

The house shuddered, and Jack tasted terror for the man. "No!"

When Robert reached the tip, the house twisted and rose, then collapsed inward. Brick crumbled, puffs of smoke and mist sprayed outward, and then the roof disappeared.

twenty-five

Jack felt the bite of Alaina's admonition as he drifted, aimlessly, helplessly, pulled by currents he couldn't see that had rendered him too weak to fight. He relived Robert's plunge into the monstrous body of water. His pitiful wails, even his taunting remarks, he understood. Eyes squeezed shut, he reviewed his foolish pride. His neglect. Hadn't Alaina told him all along she didn't need to be rich? How his pride had hurt her. He would listen now, if given another chance. He would hear her and marry her and love her.

Now, in the midst of disaster, houses didn't matter. Stoves and sewing machines and fancy clothes and *money*. Nothing mattered more than knowing those you loved were safe and well and whole.

He allowed himself the sobs when he considered he might not get another chance. He had to try, to fight as much as he could. First, he must rest. His eyes felt heavy, and he floated, numb to his surroundings and the sounds and the awful swirl of water that dragged him around.

When he finally raised his head, he thought he heard voices. He floated close to a building. People hung out the windows, arms outstretched and beckoning him. It penetrated slowly that they were calling to him.

"Over here!"

He blinked away the dullness and started to kick his feet. A familiar face came into focus, but he couldn't put a name to the man. "Hurry before you crash."

Then he felt it. A current. Sucking him out. Away from the man and his hand and the hope of a solid place to lay his head and rest. He moved his feet, and the muscles in his legs cramped. He ground his teeth against the pain and moved them anyway, wanting so much to rest, to slide away.

You can do it, Jack.

He moved his head, kicked as hard as he could. A stab of pain shot through his brain. Then hands were reaching for his board and pulling him close. He heard the grunts and groans of men, felt himself lifted.

"Bad gash on his head. Get the doc."

In what seemed minutes, someone leaned over him and said, "I'm Dr. William Matthews."

Jack closed his eyes, secure in the knowledge he was out of the waters. He breathed a heartfelt *Thank You, Lord*, and allowed himself to slip away.

❧

When Jack woke in the dark of night, he found himself in a room full of people. Some lay on the ground, moaning, their snippets of prayers punctuated by the cries of children in the high-ceilinged room. Close to the front windows as he was, Jack could see those around him, while those farther into the room were shadowed in dark gray. But the reason for the light in the pitch dark of night sickened him—fires had broken out.

He sat up and touched the single strand of cotton circling his head. A dull ache throbbed at the base of his skull. A high-pitched scream rent the air and then faded, but the sound brought Jack to his feet and made his scalp crawl.

"She's giving birth. Babies do not wait for convenient times to be born. Just as death does not rely on convenience to schedule its grim appointment. We must be ready."

It took Jack a moment to put a face to the voice. A little woman sat in a corner, her clothes in tatters. She shook in the chill air, folded her head onto her drawn-up knees, and went silent, as if the explanation wrenched the last of her strength.

Another scream rose. This one lingered long before it faded back, and within moments, the pitiful wail of a baby joined the jumble of shrieks and prayers.

Jack went to the window and tried to piece together where he was and what had happened. Not knowing where Frank was. Or Missy and Sam. Or Charlotte.

"You're awake."

Jack turned, the quick action rewarded with a roll of dull pain that clenched his stomach.

"Take it easy, son. Jack, isn't it?"

Jack could make out the outline of the man who had helped him earlier. "Dr. Matthews."

"Yes." The man inhaled deeply, and his face contorted as if in pain. "Yes. Did our newest baby wake you?"

"No. No, I just woke up."

"Rest did you good. Why don't you stay here and keep a lookout for anyone who might need help. There are still a few people out there like yourself. We fear the building might go at any time, but we can hardly ignore the needs of others."

Jack touched the bandage around his head.

"Quite a gash. I have little to help you with, but I did try to wrap the bandage and stop the flow of blood."

"Thank you. I'll help any way I can, of course."

Dr. Matthews patted his shoulder. "We'll need you, I've no doubt. It will be a long, dark night."

twenty-six

June 1, 1889

In the strange silence of morning, Jack realized the blow to his head had affected his vision. Where he could see clearly before his injury, now everything seemed cocooned in a dark haze.

Dr. Matthews checked his head again and tore a strip from a shirt left to dry overnight. "Think you can help us get everyone out?"

Jack started to nod, but the gesture sent pain into his head. "Sure."

Together, the men organized a way to get people to safety and toiled the rest of the morning lowering those he'd spent the night with through the window and out onto a pile of debris. From there another man took over guiding them from one stack of debris to another, closer to the mountains and safety.

By the time Jack had helped the last person through, his head throbbed and he felt too sick to notice the rumble of hunger his stomach sent out. He sank to the floor of the building and leaned his head on the windowsill.

"Let's get you out of here."

He gulped against the rising bile. "I can make it fine."

"You're in worse shape than most of those you helped," Dr. Matthews insisted. "There's a place over on Prospect that's rumored to have food."

Jack felt pressure on the back of his head as the doctor removed the bandage and probed the wound. "We need to get this cleaned out. Hopefully some medical supplies are on the way."

"What about you? Don't have to be a doctor to know you're hurt, too."

"I think I bruised a couple of ribs." Dr. Matthews winced. "It only hurts to breathe."

Jack allowed himself a small smile at the man's attempt at levity.

The doctor pulled Jack to his feet. "Come on."

They picked their way across the piles of wood two and three stories tall and places where water still stood.

"You have family here?" Matthews asked.

"My parents have been dead a long time, but I was engaged." He winced at the choice of words. "Her name's Alaina Morrison. She and her mother lived above Heiser's store."

The doctor shook his head. "It's all gone, Jack. Most of Washington Street just. . .washed away."

Jack inhaled the sordid, heavy air, feeling the unfairness of his life amongst so much destruction. If he stopped, if he allowed himself to think long and hard, he would break down. He had to find out about Charlotte. If she'd had warning, maybe she, too, had floated away, alive somewhere on one of the hills surrounding Johnstown. If so, he needed to find her. To learn about Missy and Sam. And Frank.

The only bright spot was his knowledge that Alaina had been spared. Now if only he could have another chance to make things right and love her as she deserved to be loved. He slipped his eyes closed and pressed his fingers against the lids as a crushing pain stabbed behind the sockets.

"Jack?"

Dr. Matthews's grip tightened his hold across Jack's shoulders. Jack felt his arm lifted and Dr. Matthews's shoulder wedged beneath his armpit as the stabbing pain receded and he fell into unconsciousness.

❧

Alaina allowed the man to cover her with a blanket.

"You'll be warmer now, Miss Morrison."

She nibbled at the piece of bread she held and shivered as much from shock as from the chill in the air. Still, God had provided her traveling companions in the form of two gentlemen, journalists determined to get to Johnstown by foot, just as she was.

Through the night, on their four-mile trek across the mountain, they peppered her with questions on the layout of Johnstown and its surrounding towns. When they arrived on the hillside in the early morning hours, and she had first laid eyes on the destruction, the chills began, sending her protectors on a mission to build a fire and find a blanket.

Her friend crouched beside her. "News is starting to trickle in, but Clarence and I will check on you when we can."

She couldn't respond, her mind unable to grasp anything more than the frightful knowledge that she might have lost everyone. *Jack. Momma. Frank. Missy. Sam.* Her head ached, and her throat burned with a fire unquenched by her tears.

Lord God. . .Jack. . .Please, God. . .Momma, Missy. . .so many. . .

She tried to touch the thought of life without Jack, of her mother caught somewhere in one of the few buildings left standing or, worse, in the acres of debris at the bridge that burned and burned and burned. When she finally broke through the shock, she had wandered along the edges of the great puddle that was now Johnstown, to help with those who'd been rescued.

She sat quietly by one man whose leg was obviously broken and tried to keep him warm. A parade of men and women passed her as she held vigil. Searching. Everyone seemed to be searching for someone. Sobs and pitiful wailing became a constant drone in Alaina's ears.

Into the evening she sat with the man, until a wagon came down to take those who were wounded to higher ground.

"There's a camp up a ways," said the farmer who stopped in front of her. "I'll take him up there."

In the fading light of early evening, Alaina saw the deep sadness carved into the lines around the farmer's eyes. "Will you take me, too?"

He nodded and waved to a man nearby. "Help me load him up."

She learned in the short trip up the hill that the farmer, Mr. Fry, lived on the crest and had seen the wave slam into Johnstown.

"Woodvale is gone. Heard say that South Fork was mostly spared, being most of the town is on the hill." She felt his stare. "You looking for your folks?"

She exhaled and pulled a tress of hair back from her face. "My mother and—" *Jack.* The name came to her tongue, but she couldn't say it out loud. Her throat closed painfully.

"You'll find them soon. No sense in thinking the worst yet. It'll freeze you up inside. These ladies up here, they might know someone, or your people might even be there."

After stepping out of the wagon, Alaina realized the short trip had caused her limbs to stiffen. She moved slowly, giving herself time to process the women.

The shrouded shapes lay in rows a few feet away from those who sipped from tins of milk or chewed on crusts of bread. One woman, a bloody, torn bandage on her head, sobbed uncontrollably. There were so many who needed help or comfort. Most needed both.

Alaina thanked the farmer and left him to unload his passenger. As she drew nearer, she scanned faces for those of her mother or Jack. She crossed her arms and rubbed along flesh pimpled from the chill air.

One of the women saw her and met her halfway. "We have some food if you're hungry."

"No." She shook her head. "I—I came to help." She swallowed. "And to find my mother, my. . .friends."

The woman's eyes went soft. "I'm Liza. We welcome the help." She motioned toward the shrouded forms. "Would you like me to come with you?"

Alaina curled into a ball and rested her head on her knees. She felt the stress of the day in every part of her body and wanted only to blink and have Johnstown return to its previous splendor. To have her mother safely beside her, piecing patterns together and basting material for a fitting. She wanted to see Mary and hear her chatter about the big city and to run in the fields with Missy and Sam.

The men were bringing another body up the hill.

Alaina swiped at the myriad of tendrils clinging to her neck and face and rose to help unload supplies from the back of Mr. Fry's wagon.

One of the women squinted up at the old farmer standing in the back of his wagon. "We can never thank you enough, Mr. Fry."

The man gave a nod. His eyes strayed out toward Johnstown, then back. "It is the very least I can do, Miss Mandy. The people of Brownstown are opening up their homes. Send them our way for the night. We'll feed 'em and make sure they have dry places to sleep and blankets against the cold. Got more of that milk there, too. And ham. Got some bread. Our women are baking up more." As he talked, he bent his back to the work of unloading the goods he'd brought down.

When the wagon was empty, they began to sort the provisions. The farmer rolled off, promising to return.

The same woman who'd thanked the farmer worked alongside Alaina. "You find your family?"

Alaina pressed her lips together. "No." She blinked and a single tear streamed down her cheek.

"I'm sorry. I tend to speak without thinking. I came down from the farm up there this morning. Seen a lot in my life, but never so much as this."

"My mother is all I have. I was to be married, but I—"

The woman placed a gentle hand on Alaina's shoulder. "Please don't explain. Rest a bit while we finish here."

She shook her head. "It's best for me to keep moving."

"Suit yourself. I surely welcome the help. Looks like more people are heading this way. Word is getting out that we have food."

Alaina's sorrow overflowed as she stared out at Johnstown. "We realize how very little we truly need to survive at times like this."

twenty-seven

June 2, 1889

Alaina wiped her eyes, the weariness and smoke causing them to water. Not to mention the stream of grief that she witnessed as loved ones identified the bodies of their mothers, fathers, children. . .and friends. She bit her lip hard and forced away the memory of Mary's serene expression. The girl's body had been brought in late afternoon, and the reality of her friend's death had chipped away at the last bits of strength that kept her functioning. She'd been grateful then for Mandy's embrace that not only held her upright but also helped take the edge off her grief.

A new stream of people moved into the campsite, while men worked to build shelters for families who needed them. Still, the long line of those sick and hurt had continued to grow with no end in sight.

"The men are getting together to see what's to be done. We can't function under these circumstances for much longer. I did hear we've finally got contact and a train brought in supplies. If we can just. . ." Mandy's words faded, and Alaina knew her friend saw what she had seen, the new stream of people headed their way.

She pressed her friend's hand and forced a smile. "We'll make it. I know we will."

"Oh!" Mandy pressed her hand to her chest.

Alaina followed her friend's gaze and saw nothing to incite such a reaction. The line of limping, wet, bedraggled people hadn't changed.

"It's Dr. Matthews. He came to see my sister when she was so sick and"—she clasped her hands together—"I know he'll be such a help to those who are ill."

Alaina, still unsure which man was the doctor, moved to help with the new wave of hurt and hungry.

Mandy passed her and went toward Dr. Matthews and his companion, one helping the other.

Alaina's attention was diverted by the crying of a naked child and the swollen eyes of a mother, dressed in rags and shivering. "Let me take the child," she admonished the woman. She helped the lady to a spot on the ground, near a fire that a young boy of ten had diligently fed all through the long night. Alaina knelt next to the woman and child, at a loss for helping her other than to offer the meager bread and a tin of milk. "I'll try to find something to bundle the child in and get you some bread and milk."

The woman reached for her baby, then curled her body around the child in a silent offer to share what little body heat she had. If she couldn't get him covered soon, the child would catch pneumonia.

Lord, please send us blankets soon.

Alaina pulled at her skirts as she rose to avoid tripping over the hem and turned to find Mandy behind her.

"Dr. Matthews is going to do what he can for those here."

Alaina glanced behind Mandy and saw the doctor leaning over the man he'd helped in. His shirt was little more than a strip of cloth across his chest. The strip around the man's head was dirty and caked with blood. Their supply of well water had dwindled to nothing in little time, but Mr. Fry had assured them other wagons were headed their way. As soon as she could, she would tend to the man's wound.

That's when Alaina caught the profile of the doctor's companion. Her heart beat hard as the man raised his head. The hair. The shape of his nose. His silhouette against the lightness of the sky. . .

"Jack!"

His head jerked her way, but he didn't move.

She stumbled over the young mother's foot and almost

plunged straight into Mandy, but she kept going. "Jack!"

Within a few steps of him, she stopped. Her throat closed over a tight wad of tears.

In one swift motion, he swept to his feet. He blinked, then blinked again. The shine of tears in his eyes. "Alaina?"

She went into his arms then and felt his strong arms press her to him.

"Alaina?"

"I'm here, Jack."

He buried his face in her hair, and she felt his chest jerk before the first sob, a harsh, almost animal-like wail, grated against her ear and brought her own tears to the surface.

◆

Robert's plea for help and his inability to rescue him in time. The gash on his head and the long, terrible night that followed. All of it seemed to fade away as Jack held Alaina close. Her softness took the edge off hard reality and sent a breath of relief through every tension-filled limb.

Her tears mingled with his as he stroked her hair.

In the minutes that passed, he absorbed her presence like the starving man he had become since the water had wiped out Johnstown. He pulled back, wanting so much to see her face. Needing to trace the outline of her nose and see the dark eyes he so loved. But her face wouldn't come into focus.

She grasped his elbows. "You're hurt."

"But I'm alive."

He felt the quiver of her body, and fresh tears were falling. "I was so scared. Momma?"

He shook his head. "I don't know. The entire street was wiped out. Everything. It could be days before we know."

She went into his arms again, and he cradled her head against his chest. He wanted to say something comforting, but the words didn't come. He satisfied himself with the knowledge that Alaina was safe. She was here, and hope filled him anew.

But eventually, his injury took its toll, and weakness gripped him. He pulled away from her.

"Jack?"

He lowered himself to the ground and leaned his arms on bent knees. "Just need to. . .sit." Bile rose hot in his throat, and he leaned over. He felt the tug on the bandage around his head and heard Alaina's words, but she seemed to be talking from a great distance. He strained to make sense of everything, but he couldn't.

"I'll take care of you,." Alaina's voice reassured.

Jack gave in to her ministrations, knowing he would be safe now.

twenty-eight

Through the day, Alaina sat beside Jack as much as she could. Though Mandy insisted she stay near him, Alaina knew the women were pushed to their limits offering comfort and the little bit of food they could. Besides, Jack remained unconscious, and rather than worry about the implications of his unresponsiveness, she was determined to keep busy.

When she had the chance to grab a few minutes to talk to Mandy, the news was better than she'd hoped.

"The train got through this morning, and people are arriving to help us out." Mandy ran a hand over her flat hair and swiped at her left cheek, leaving a smudge of dirt.

"We'll have help soon. Blankets and water and food."

"Yes." Mandy closed her eyes. "Dr. Matthews and Dr. Lowman are setting up a temporary hospital on Bedford. They'll want to take the worst cases over at some point."

As Jack slept on, Alaina's worry mounted. Knowing the doctors were pressed for time and that there were far too many to care for between the two of them, she did her best to help prepare the patients to be moved. When she came to a lone woman, her hand clutching a scrap of material, Alaina felt a deep sorrow. Almost forty-eight hours since the flood and the lady's arrival in the camp and she still could not be coaxed to say a word or take food and drink. She bent close to the woman and held the mug out. "Would you take a drink for me?"

The only response was a gentle caressing of the fabric.

Alaina set the tin mug aside and placed a gentle hand on the thin forearm. "Could I see the lovely material?" When those words were out, she cast about for something more to add. "It must mean a great deal to you. My mother was"—she steeled herself against the unconscious use of that word and continued—"*is* a seamstress and loves material and making dresses."

Still nothing.

Ever so slowly, Alaina reached out and unfolded the tiny corner of the material to see the subtle pattern of small flowers against a dirty azure background. She processed the tattered edge, as if it had been torn. "It's a beautiful shade of blue. Did you have it made into a dress or do it up yourself?" She realized the color of the lady's dress, although blue, did not match that of the scrap she held. Her heart clenched in compassion, and she raised a hand to stroke the strands of hair back out of the woman's dark brown eyes. "One day I'd like to have a dress made of that color. Blue always makes me think of sunshine and birds. I suspect a lot of people enjoy blue."

The woman shifted a bit on the hard ground.

Alaina picked up the tin. "Would you like a drink? Mr. Fry brought it down from his farm. He's going to try and bring more bread and blankets. If I find one with the color blue in it, I'll be sure to bring it to you. Would you like that?"

No response.

With a sigh, Alaina rose from her spot next to the woman and groped for something more to say to draw out the shattered soul. Alaina turned to check on the next person when she heard the slightest whisper.

"Bluebirds."

She turned and stared down at the woman. Only when she knelt beside her did Alaina see the stream of wetness along the woman's cheek.

She released her clutch on the material and raised it to her cheek. "Bluebirds."

"What did you say to her?" Mandy's voice floated over Alaina's shoulder. She tilted her head to see her friend.

"I'm not sure. I mentioned the color blue and how it reminded me of birds." Alaina leaned toward the woman and again tried to press her to take a drink.

To her surprise the woman parted her lips and drank deeply,

though she turned her head away after one swallow.

Satisfied, Alaina patted the woman's shoulder and got to her feet. In the waning daylight, the chill of the gray day would give way to another cold night. She hated to see the people struggling to stay warm while dealing with such chaos and deep loss.

She stepped over the inert forms of the injured and reached Jack's side. A sigh escaped as she sank to the ground next to him. With gentle fingers, she picked up his hand and twined her fingers with his. She'd left him to pursue her mother's dream for her. She understood now that her mother's dream could not be hers. But her mother had been right in one very important way—she could not promise to marry a man who thought more of wealth than he did of her. She recalled all the broken promises and empty evenings when Jack's promised visit turned out to be another study in loneliness for her. As much as she hated how she had broken the engagement, she would do it again. For her own sake. And if he was the man she thought he was, he would understand that decision.

Watching the rise and fall of his chest, and the stroke of his lashes against his unshaven cheeks, desperation rose in her. It would be so easy to ignore her common sense and marry him, if for no other reason than he was all she seemed to have.

Where was her mother? How would she find her in all this? Alaina's stomach churned.

God, how do I find Momma? Where do I look? And Missy and Sam. Frank.

It was all so confusing, yet she thanked Him for the miracle of Jack's life, and as she did, she squeezed his hand to her breast, then kissed the tips of his chilled fingers.

twenty-nine

June 3, 1889

Jack knew he should open his eyes. The angel that sat next to him kept saying his name and stroking a soft hand along his brow, but his head hurt so much. Pain so bad he knew any light would grind the ache in his head to a sharper point. So he kept his eyes shut.

"You know, Jack, I think it's time you woke up and stopped giving this young woman of yours so much grief."

In his mind, he smiled. Dr. Matthews's voice. He squeezed the small hand nestled in his and decided if he couldn't open his eyes, at least he could talk. "Hurts too much."

"A big, tough guy such as yourself is afraid of a little headache?"

Jack pursed his lips. He heard the quiet challenge and felt the soft poke of the man's words. Just as he had worked up the courage to pry his eyes open, another voice, more gravelly than the first, called Dr. Matthews away.

"Jack?"

He turned his head toward Alaina's voice. "Hey."

"Do you need a drink?"

"Yes." Within minutes he felt the press of a cup to his lips, but the strain of sitting up caused his head to pound harder and brought a wave of nausea with it. He relaxed back and rolled with the pain, swallowing convulsively over the urge to throw up.

Alaina dabbed his head with a cool cloth.

He wanted so much to ask her to put one at the base of his skull where the pain was most acute. He pulled air into his lungs and let it out long and slow.

148

"Dr. Lowman sewed up the gash in the back of your head."

He didn't remember it. A good thing, he was sure. "How long?"

"You've been unconscious for two days. The doctors established a temporary hospital on Bedford Street, so that's where you are now."

A question swirled in his brain. Something he wanted to ask, but the more he tried to bring it into focus, the more it eluded him, until he finally surrendered to the fog permeating his mind and fell asleep.

৵

June 5, 1889

Joy surged through Alaina as she embraced young Sam despite the awkwardness of his position on the bed. "Sam, look who is here."

Behind them, Missy's squeals filled the air. Sam turned his head, and his eyes lit up when he saw his sister in his father's arms.

Alaina heaved a sigh of satisfaction. When Sam and Missy, bedraggled and dirty, and Sam with a badly bruised and broken leg, had been brought into the hospital late Sunday, Alaina had immediately registered their names in case Frank had survived the flood and was looking for them. Then she had prayed. To see him now, here, with his children close, brought a deep, abiding peace to her.

Frank, propped on crutches against the wall, didn't bother to shield the tears of relief that streamed down his cheeks as he clung to Missy. He raised his head and shook it back and forth. "I don't know what to say." The man lowered himself beside Sam and held his son's hand, stroking the hair from the boy's face.

"Joy unspeakable." Alaina smiled.

"With all the suffering. . ." Frank's voice caught and with his free hand he pulled Missy closer and buried his face in her hair.

He didn't have to finish the statement. Alaina understood. Everyone who found a missing loved one understood the ecstasy and the bitterness of realizing others were not so fortunate. It still wrenched her heart to see a woman fling herself across the identified body of a husband or child. She closed her eyes against the vision. Working to care for those in the hospital, she'd seen it too many times.

Sam shifted on the bed. Fever raged hot, turning his skin a bright pink, but the doctor had hope the boy would pull through. And despite his leg trapping him in debris, the workers had done their best to free the limb without inflicting more damage. What he needed most was food and water and rest.

Frank raised his head. "I couldn't lie there not knowing and started searching right away, sure I'd lost them when I heard that Washington Street had pretty much disappeared. I must have passed out, though, because I woke up and was being carried somewhere. I don't remember too much after that. Someone told me to check at the clearinghouse and there they were listed—" His voice choked off.

Alaina understood his emotion. "Sam said my mother got them to the attic and went down for something. Missy wanted to follow her, but Sam jerked her along just as the wave hit them."

"Your mother?" Frank asked.

She could only shake her head.

"I'm sorry, Alaina. I'll check the clearinghouse and post office on Adams and Main. People are registering all the time." The big man's expression radiated compassion. "I'll head there now."

"You can't. You're hurt, too," she protested.

"I'm big and I've had time to heal. Probably the lying around is making me hurt more than the injury."

"Can I go?" Missy piped up.

"I'll need your help." He got to his feet and pulled the crutch close, then reached to tousle Missy's already-mussed hair. "Some of the roads are still hard to get through, though. Think you're up to it?"

The little girl nodded a solemn nod and clung to his outstretched hand. "Will Sam be all right, Pa?"

Only Alaina understood the worry in Frank's gaze as it scanned Sam's face and then drifted to his heavily bandaged leg. "Give him a few days and he'll be chasing you around Green Hill."

Alaina paced down the aisle to catch a breath of fresh air. So much had happened in so few days. Supplies and money had come in from all over, yet still people suffered, though now more in spirit than in body.

Out the window, the bonfires raged on, their acrid scent scorching the air. Though needful, it still sickened Alaina to watch as dead horses and cows were cremated in the hot flames.

"Alaina?"

She turned from the morbid sight to the voice behind her.

A woman she'd not seen before spoke. "The young man is asking for you."

She nodded, and the woman scurried in a different direction. When she got to Jack's side, it pleased her to see his eyes open. At long last.

His blue gaze swept in her direction and settled on her, though a crease in his brow brought Dr. Matthews's warning to mind.

"Are you still having trouble with your vision?" she asked as she scooped his hand into hers.

"Hard to see you clear. Must have hit harder than I thought."

She brushed her fingertips along his brow, glad no fever seemed present. "Does your head still hurt?"

He winced and licked his lips. "Not as much. Bearable."

"Can you eat something?"

"I am hungry." His eyes closed, and he rolled his head away from her, but not before she caught the way his lips twitched and the working of his jaw. His voice came out raspy. "What if my vision doesn't clear?"

"Jack, hush. You're awake. Alive. Do you know what a miracle that is for me? I thought I'd lost everyone."

His sobs were silent, but she felt every one of them reverberate deep in her soul. She understood that his pain reached far beyond his vision. There were a million questions she wanted to ask him about the whole incident, but she held back as she knew she should. He, like so many others she'd helped in the last few days, had endured so much. More than she could comprehend. They needed time to heal on the inside.

Alaina gripped Jack's hand harder and stroked his brow. "I'm here, Jack."

When he quieted, he rolled his head to face her and swiped at the signs of his tears.

Alaina batted his hand away and stroked the shiny paths glistening along his cheeks. "We'll get through this. You've already come so far."

He touched her cheek, his fingertips rough against her skin.

She nuzzled her face against his hand.

"I love you."

The words melted her resolve to be strong, and the warmth in his eyes brought heat to her cheeks. She straightened in the chair and leaned forward, determined to avoid a conversation best left for another time and place. "We'll talk later. Just rest and get better."

She shifted mental gears and told him about Frank, Missy and Sam. This seemed to lift Jack's spirits, and when he finally closed his eyes again, Alaina found comfort in the fact that she'd given him good news.

thirty

June 8, 1889

Jack pushed himself to sit up. His head didn't pound like it used to, and his vision had cleared, but he still felt fuzzy. Probably from not eating and from lying around for so many days. He made up his mind that he would walk out of the hospital that day.

Across from him, Sam slept on despite the usual noise. The noise. He'd be glad to go to sleep and not be awakened by groans or grunts or the usual hospital cacophony. With great effort, he swung his legs off the edge of the bed and hesitated. His world spun, then settled.

"Taking off?"

Jack tried to focus on the person at the end of his bed. *Frank.* "If they're putting you in here, I am."

"Well, they're not." Frank spread his arms. "And no more crutches."

"Wonderful. Now help me off this bed and out that door."

Frank's chuckle reached Jack's ears. "You think that's wise? Doctors might have something to say about it."

"They won't miss me, and I'm sure they could use the space."

Jack tensed his muscles to push himself up, but Frank's hand clamped down on his shoulder. "You're an idiot, Kelly. You've not been vertical in almost seven days, and you're going to try to just walk out of here. You'll be on the floor so fast you'll—"

Jack tried to shrug his friend's hand off his shoulder and push forward, but whatever Frank was, he wasn't weak.

"You should at least wait for Alaina."

Which Jack translated to mean, *"Maybe she'll say something to penetrate that thick skull.*" He chuckled and relaxed. "You win. I'll behave."

"Good. Now, before she gets here—"

"You going to lecture me again about treating her badly? Because I can tell you that being flat on my back, seeing all the destruction, surviving, has taught me a lot. I've been a fool."

Frank pounded his shoulder, though not with his usual force. "You sure have, and I'm glad you've jerked to your senses. But that wasn't what I was going to say."

Jack squeezed his eyes shut. *Oh, brother.*

"I heard someone say there's quite a few people up in Brownstown who haven't registered. I'm headed up there to see if Charlotte might be among them."

Jack hoped for Alaina's sake that she was. Though he and Charlotte seemed at odds, with Alaina caught in the middle, Jack didn't wish anything bad on her, for her sake as well as for Alaina's. Losing her mother would break Alaina's heart.

Though he'd never given much thought to Charlotte's disapproval of him, he saw now what Frank had tried to tell him months ago. People's lives mold their beliefs, just as his father's continual failings and living in poverty had molded his need to succeed. . .to be rich. Even to the exclusion of loving Alaina as he should. God had showed him so much in such a short span of time.

&

The crude shelter creaked and groaned with the breezes. Alaina pulled her hair back into a low bun to mask the need for a good hair-washing. She stretched and tried to work the soreness from muscles not used to sleeping on hard surfaces. Oh, to soak in a nice tub of water. She'd give anything for the luxury.

As she crossed from Prospect Hill into Johnstown, Alaina's spirits rose. The townspeople, with a lot of help from outsiders, worked hard to remove debris and build temporary housing. Clara Barton had arrived on the fifth of June, and already hotels were being built under her direction, along with Red

Cross tents to serve as hospitals. Still, even with the progress brought by relief efforts, the townspeople seemed cloaked in melancholia. *Time heals all.*

She rounded the edge of the temporary hospital as nurses and doctors were readying people for transfer to the Red Cross tents. Down the row, she could see Frank standing beside Jack. Relief tweaked at her mind to see Jack sitting up, yet the sight also became tinged with worry when she recognized the stubborn set of Jack's jaw and the hand Frank had on his shoulder.

As she closed in on the two, she overheard Frank's intentions of going up to Brownstown to search for her mother. She detoured to Sam's bed and found him sound asleep. She pulled the blanket up higher on the boy's chest and smoothed the chestnut hair back from his smooth brow.

Frank caught sight of her first. "Just telling this brute he needed to lay himself down before he slid off onto the floor. He's got it into his head that he can just hop to his feet and walk out of here."

"He's a bully." Jack reached up to grasp her hand. "You'll protect me though, won't you?"

The warmth of his hand sent her heart into a canter. "I'll protect you." She sent a wink to Frank then scowled at Jack. "Now lie down and be a good patient."

Jack groaned and squeezed her hand. "Yes, ma'am. Somehow it's sweeter coming from you."

"Let's see what the doctor says before you try anything heroic. I do think it's a good idea that you sit up more often."

"I want to get out of here and help out."

"Making sure you're strong enough not to fall down face-first would help everyone out a lot," Frank inserted.

Jack glared at Frank.

Alaina laughed. "You two are worse than Missy and Sam."

"I heard that."

Everyone's attention went to the bed next to Jack, where a sleepy-eyed Sam watched the group. Frank went to his son and hugged him. The two fell into quiet chatter that swelled Alaina's heart. She didn't think she could have borne losing Sam or Missy.

"Am I that easily dismissed?"

She laughed down at Jack. "No."

He raised her hand to his chest.

"Not at all."

"Tell me what you've been up to. What it's really like out there."

The warm feeling melted away. "Why don't you concentrate on getting better?"

His thumb caressed her knuckles. "I hear so much. Bits and pieces. I'm stronger now though, and I want to know what I can do to help. How bad is it?"

Her lip quivered, and she willed herself not to cry. All this time and she'd not given herself much chance to grieve, not that she'd had much time with all the work to be done. But now, looking into Jack's soft blue eyes, the core of self-control crumbled, and she choked on a sob.

thirty-one

Jack saw the warning signals that tears were impending and pushed himself up. He reached to pull her into his embrace, grateful the dizziness had eased. He pressed his cheek to the top of her head and absorbed her emotions. It must have been very bad. Having seen the great swell of water and having fought its current for so long, he should have known, yet he had somehow held hope.

Sam's eyes were round with concern, and Jack gave the boy a smile of reassurance to erase the worry from both Sam and Frank's minds.

Eventually, Alaina pulled back. "I shouldn't be crying. Some have lost everyone in their families."

Jack pressed his finger to her lips. "Worry for your mother is mixed in with those tears." He stroked the hair from her face. "Besides, I'm hanging on to you as much as you're hanging on to me. I admit the world is still a little shaky."

She pressed a hand against his chest. "Lie down. I don't want you to—"

He caught her wrist. "I'm fine, Alaina. I promise."

"But if you make yourself sick, they might—"

"Shh. Listen to me." His words were taut with urgency. "I want to get out of here. Walk with me a bit so I can get my strength up."

She stared into his eyes, and he saw the silent plea in the brown depths. "It's not something you want to see. Johnstown is. . .gone."

"I've already seen some of it, though it was blurry." He wanted her to understand. "I need to feel a part of what's going on out there."

She didn't protest as he slid to the edge of the bed and let his feet dangle and then touch the floor. As soon as his feet made contact, needles of pain shot into his ankles, and he froze his expression so Alaina would not pick up on the pain the effort generated.

When it finally dissipated, he got to his feet. The room spun and dipped. Despite his best efforts, his weakness was evident because Alaina was there in a second, helping to support him. Jack inhaled deeply and let his breath out in a measured exhale.

"Jack, are you sure this is a good idea?"

He pasted on a smile. "If I fall down, just cover me with a blanket."

"How's your head feel?"

"Better than it has." He didn't mention the fact that it throbbed terribly now that he was upright.

At Alaina's insistence, he took small steps, knowing her eyes were glued to his face for any sign of weakness.

Lord, help me to do this so she can stop worrying about me.

When they finally reached the entry, Jack prompted Alaina to keep going. "I'm doing pretty good. Let's get outside." As soon as he emerged into the sunshine, a myriad of odors assaulted his nostrils and almost drove him to his knees.

Alaina immediately jumped into action and directed him toward an empty crate. "Sit."

"It's terrible," he murmured.

"It's worse up on the hills. What you see down here are mostly visitors who have come in to help. Up on the hill where I've been helping, that's where the people—the survivors— are. They're like lost souls, hollow and empty. Some just stare, others cry, but all of them are afraid, constantly searching for those they lost."

"I want to see more." His mind went to Robert. It felt like such a dream. He would never forget Robert's face or the terror of being pulled by an unseen current.

"Are you sure?"

He nodded. "Yes, I'm sure. And there's something else I need to tell you."

Alaina listened as Jack talked. At first she had thought he'd simply felt a need to ease his own mind about the nightmare he'd endured, but then his tone changed, and he visibly tensed.

He talked of his ride through Johnstown on his simple plank of wood, being twisted by the ebb and flow of the water and pounded against objects in his way. He paused for breath.

She touched his cheek. "You can tell me the rest later. It's all over with, Jack. You're safe."

He squeezed his eyes shut, and his breathing became ragged. When he pressed her hand against his cheek, it was with greater force than necessary. "You don't understand, Alaina. It was terrible. And there was someone I tried to save. I tried to get him to jump—" His voice broke, and his free hand clenched into a fist. "I never understood what you meant by *'people mean more than things'* until I saw him."

She froze, mesmerized by the power of his emotion.

"It all came to me. The job, the inventions. Forgetting you. Saving people—" His jaw clenched, and a storm of emotion darkened his eyes.

"Because you couldn't do anything?"

"No. Because I could, would have, but the pull of the water was too strong. I felt like a rag doll being pulled apart and tossed. I called to him to jump, but he sneered at me. He was afraid. I could hear his fear. Taste it."

Alaina's mind shuffled through a list of people whom Jack considered friends. "One of the men at Cambria?"

"No." His face contorted. "No. Robert. I was trying to save Robert."

Alaina sat stunned. She turned her hand in his and twined them.

"He wouldn't listen. The house moved and it. . .it *twisted*. My head hurt so much, but I knew I had to get Robert off that roof."

Her heart lifted as she began to understand what it was Jack was trying to tell her.

"It sucked me away from him and I—I don't know. I think I yelled at him one more time to jump, but it was gone. He was gone." He released her hand and covered his face. "I floated for a long time, and all I could think was that I'd been so wrong. So dumb. Selfish." He lowered his hands, his red, swollen eyes searching hers. "I knew, then, how much Frank was right."

"Frank?"

For the first time, the semblance of a smile curved Jack's lips. "Yes. He told me I was an idiot. That I was treating you badly. I kept defending myself and everything that I was doing, thinking that was somehow more important. Having money. . ." He lifted his eyes to the devastation. "I see it now."

"Oh, Jack."

He turned to her and cupped her face. "Can you forgive me? For all those times I put riches ahead of your heart?"

"You thought what you were doing was right."

Jack pressed a finger against her lips. "Don't defend me. I hurt you. Not once, not twice, but again and again and again. So determined to have money that I never once listened to what you told me so often. You didn't want to be rich."

She pressed her hand against his. "I still don't."

"Then marry me, Alaina. Marry me, and this time I'll get it right."

thirty-two

June 9, 1889

After another good night's sleep, Jack accompanied Alaina to the clearinghouse again. They scoured the names for any sign of Charlotte Morrison, but still no one had registered by that name.

Alaina closed her eyes in defeat.

"You left directions where you're staying. Frank'll find you. Give the rescue workers and Frank some more time," Jack murmured.

He was right, of course. She'd made sure a nurse at the temporary hospital and one at the Red Cross hospital knew where to find her, but days had passed, and she was more worried than ever that Frank had lost heart because the news wasn't good.

And then there was Jack's proposal. He had recognized her hesitation and been sensitive to her reasoning in waiting for news of her mother. But his actions went a long way toward proving his sincerity. He sought her out every morning to check on her, then went off to work at the bridge to help clean up the terrible mass of wreckage.

If only she could say "yes" and feel clear, but she didn't.

"You've got that look again," Jack said softly, his eyes shining their concern. "I told you, Alaina, I'll wait for you. You're right to want news of your mother."

She sighed. "It seems so wrong to feel happy in times like these."

Jack's gaze drifted toward the wreckage at the bridge and over to Cambria Iron. She saw his Adam's apple bob and knew he understood.

Even almost a week since the tragedy, there was still so

much grief and chaos. Fear of disease ran rampant. The stench in the air was almost unbearable. So many people had come in from other areas of the country that familiar faces were too few and far between.

Unless you went to the morgue or hospital.

Alaina patted Jack's arm. "I need to check on Sam, then get over to the tent."

Jack nodded and touched her cheek briefly. "You know where I'll be."

She smiled at the tenderness in his eyes, and thankfulness washed through her that God had spared Jack. "I know." She paused, then said, "I love you, Jack Kelly."

&

When Jack came to the tent for supper, he took a moment to watch Alaina, as he had watched her all those days ago at the South Fork Fishing and Hunting Club.

She bent next to a small child and tried to coax a smile from the boy's solemn mouth. She plucked bread from the dishpan she carried and set it on the table. The boy nibbled on the edges and continued to watch Alaina as she talked, engaging the small group of children in some story or another.

His day had been long. The dynamite used to blow apart the debris at the bridge had done the job, but the mess had to be hauled away, long, muscle-aching work. He wanted nothing more than to sleep. To make things worse, his head still beat a dull throb against his skull, making every movement that much more painful.

But watching Alaina, he took comfort in her beauty and gentleness, her faith and the fervency with which she worked. Why hadn't he seen it before? She emptied herself to help other people and never expected much in return. She'd done it by loving him, even as he had shunned her.

When Alaina spotted him, she gave him bread, while another woman set a succulent slice of ham in front of him. Yet another lady arrived to ladle coffee into a tin cup.

He caught Alaina's eye. "You'll sit with me, right?"

"I can't. There are so many others who need—"

The woman ladling out the coffee nodded toward another girl. "Liz just came in. Take a break and talk to the nice young man." Her eyes held a twinkle as she stared between Alaina and Jack. "It'll do us all some good to see that life goes on."

Jack took his time eating, the background noise of hammers and axes, whistles and bells, and the crackling of the bonfires a constant reminder of the tragedy. Still, Jack was thankful for the noise and preferred to think of what it meant. Progress. Rebuilding.

He savored every bite and every minute he could be with Alaina. But no matter how comforted he felt in her presence, another harsh reality kept nibbling at him. What would he do? Cambria would be up and running again, he was sure, but did he want to stay here? It seemed right to start over. Fresh. Away from the misery. If Charlotte lived, they could take her with them. If not, it might be even greater wisdom for him to get Alaina away from here.

But where?

"Money is pouring in from all over to help Johnstown rebuild," Alaina offered.

"So I've heard. They're paying the new men two dollars a day."

Alaina shifted in her seat and poked a bite of ham with her fork. "What will it be like after all this? Will Johnstown be the same?"

"I think that's the question on everyone's mind. It's been on mine a lot."

"Do you want to work for Cambria again?"

He thought of the promotion and of Robert's attitude when he got it over Jack. Where hot anger used to consume him at the thought of being passed over, and where once his anger spilled out on Robert, now there seemed nothing but a chasm, devoid of all feeling save one. Sorrow.

It dawned on him then that he didn't know the answers. No one did. But his faith would carry him through each day. One at a time.

"All I know right now is that I want to help. To see people rebuild and get back on their feet. From there, I'll let the Lord lead."

His peripheral vision caught a familiar figure. He turned in time to see Frank duck into the tent and gaze around at the people. Jack raised his hand to indicate to his friend where they sat. He flicked a glance at Alaina and saw the instant strain tighten her lips.

The big man negotiated through the tables and dropped into a chair beside Jack.

"It's about time you showed your face. You've had Alaina worried."

Frank grimaced and rubbed his leg. "It's been a long haul. I stopped to help some along the way, and it delayed me. When I got there, it took me a while to go 'round and see who of the Johnstown folk was there." His eyes shifted to Alaina. Dark and piercing.

Jack tensed.

"I found your mother."

Alaina gasped and closed her eyes.

Frank rushed on. "But it's not good, Alaina. She's. . ." The big man licked his lips and stabbed a panicked look at Jack.

Alaina opened her eyes. A question hung there.

"She doesn't remember anything, and she doesn't say much. It's like it stole something from her."

Jack reached a hand out to clasp Alaina's, but she pushed to her feet, her face set. "I must go see her. Frank, you'll take me to her. Jack?"

It seemed to him in that moment that she would shatter completely.

"I'll take you there," Frank promised.

Jack rose and rounded the end of the table. He stood close to Alaina and pressed her cold hands between his warm ones. "Seeing you will bring her back. I'm sure of it, sweetheart."

thirty-three

Despite Jack and Alaina's efforts, her mother remained cloaked in silence. She lowered her hand from her mother's forehead and hugged herself before glancing over at Jack. "Can you think of anything else to try?"

He shook his head. There was an edge of desperation in Alaina's voice that tugged at his heart. He'd been startled by Alaina's mother's appearance. Her once-full figure had thinned to little more than bone.

Mrs. Bledsoe, the farmer's wife who had so kindly cared for Charlotte, could shed little light on her condition. "When she came here, she was like that. Just wandering. Must have been three days ago that Ben found her and brought her here. She's not ate more than a piece of bread, or said two words put together." The woman's brown eyes were solemn. "Seems I've seen the same look on many other faces lately. Such a tragedy."

The woman had left them alone, with Alaina chattering at her mother, sharing details of her trip to Pittsburgh. Seeing Pitcairn's private car. The way the people dressed. The noise of the city. And on and on. But all her efforts failed and now she looked to him.

It struck Jack as a deep irony that Alaina, who knew how much her mother disliked him, would think he might be able to penetrate the wall Charlotte had retreated behind. What could he say? His heart beat hard as he knelt. *Lord, grant me wisdom.*

"Hi, Mrs. Morrison. Alaina and I are going on a picnic and want to take you along. If you don't mind, Frank and Missy will join us. It'll be fun."

That was it. His mind shut down, and he couldn't think of

another thing to say, so he swept to his feet and faced Alaina, keeping his voice low. "Would you mind asking Mrs. Bledsoe if she could spare a bit of food?" He fished out a few coins and pressed them into Alaina's palm. "Give these to her. Perhaps they'll help."

"But what good will a picnic do?"

Jack didn't really know. "I thought maybe if we could be together, normal again, maybe it would help her. We'll go out onto the other side of the hill, away from Johnstown, where the view is nice."

Alaina nodded. "Yes. I think it might help. Everything that happened is too much. It's the same sense I got with one of the women I ministered to on the hill."

Jack squeezed her hand, then released it. "Good. And Alaina. . ."

She caught the tender light in his eyes.

"We'll pray."

❧

The Bledsoes offered Alaina a room to stay with her mother. Upon hearing that Charlotte was a seamstress, it was Mrs. Bledsoe's idea to gather together a few scraps and a needle and put them into Charlotte's fingers. "Make her feel normal again," the farmer's wife reasoned.

At first Alaina noticed little things. Her mother ate a bit more, and she would massage the material between her fingers, and those things gave Alaina hope.

In the evenings, Jack would come up with Frank, Missy, and a mending Sam, and they would help Alaina take her mother to the little section of woods that had become their special spot. They did their best to keep the conversation away from news of Johnstown.

In the wooded spot, surrounded by a giggling Sam and Missy and watching as her mother watched the children, Alaina allowed the worry to erode her confidence.

Jack leaned forward and tapped her head. "You're thinking too much. You've got that worried wrinkle between your eyes."

She leaned back against him, allowing him to support her weight. "Sometimes I wonder if she'll ever smile again. Or laugh. Even do her sewing. Aunt Jo wants me to bring her to Pittsburgh."

"She's a kind woman, but I think you're going to be your mother's best chance of recovery. We should stay together."

"Do you think we should all go out to Pittsburgh? She wouldn't mind."

Jack didn't answer for so long that she finally shifted to look over her shoulder at him. Blue eyes captured hers. A small smile quivered on his lips.

Alaina became aware of the fact they'd spent very little time without being surrounded by her mother or Frank and the children. "Why don't we go for a walk?"

"A most brilliant idea."

Alaina laughed and shifted away from him.

He swept to his feet, steadying her rise and retaining his grip on her hand.

Frank's eyes smiled over at them from where he sat talking to Charlotte.

Jack chuckled and whispered to Alaina, "I think he approves."

They walked in silence. Alaina noted the change in direction, away from the Bledsoes' farm, and wasn't surprised when they came out on the hill overlooking Johnstown. Though still terribly scarred and riddled with debris, progress had been made.

"Will it ever be the same?" she whispered.

"In many ways, no. But change doesn't mean it's better or worse. Only different."

A cool breeze washed by her, and she leaned her head back to stare up at the sky. "It seems so strange that life goes on despite everything."

Jack didn't seem to hear. He walked on a few steps more and stopped, his body silhouetted against the sky.

She studied him and realized his shirt looked new and his suspenders, though frayed, weren't nearly as gnarled as the last pair. Even his trousers were less tattered. People had sent in used clothing from all over. "There must be a terrible need for clothing," she murmured to herself, as an idea dawned. If she could manage to secure some bolts of material, she could, with Mrs. Bledsoe's help, put together clothes for the victims. But her thoughts stopped there only briefly. Jack's posture let her know that something was wrong. "Jack?"

He faced her. "I have something to tell you."

She swallowed. Maybe in the time she'd been so preoccupied with her mother he had found someone else down in Johnstown. But no, it couldn't be. Jack loved her.

He advanced on her with an amused expression. "You've got that worried line again. Why?"

Embarrassed, she looked away. "I thought you were going to tell me you'd found someone else?" But it came out more a question than a statement, and she cringed.

Jack's hand captured her chin and tilted her face back toward him, his blue eyes darkened with disappointment. "How could you think that?"

"We haven't had much time together." She flushed. "Your clothes look new."

Jack stared down at his shirt. "A man gets some clothes from one of the shipments, and you think I'm dressing up for another woman?"

Alaina stamped her foot. "Don't you dare laugh at me."

"I'm not laughing. Really. I know you've been under a lot of stress. Everyone has." He put some distance between them. "There's something that's happened that we need to talk about."

❧

Jack knew he was being vague, but he didn't know how to suggest what he felt God had been nudging him to do. He'd wrestled with the ever-stronger urging of his spirit for two weeks, and he felt exhausted from the mental struggle.

He drew a strengthening breath. "It's ironic, really, everything that has happened in these last few days." He grimaced. "But let me start at the beginning. After the flood, as I worked at the bridge and around Johnstown, I kept wondering if I could go back to Cambria Iron. They're calling some of the men back and trying to get in full swing. Part of me wants to stay here and see Johnstown rebuilt, but then your mother is so ill, and I wondered if it would be wiser to take her away from here."

"I've thought the same thing," Alaina offered.

Hearing that made it easier and lessened Jack's fear. "But then there's you and me. And money." He swallowed. "You see, the plans I turned in right before the flood hit were looked over, and the boss thinks they might work. He called me into a meeting yesterday and gave me a nice sum."

"That's. . .wonderful news." But Alaina's words were wooden, devoid of happiness, and he thought he understood the sudden flicker in her eyes.

He licked his lips. "When I had that money in my hand, I felt such satisfaction, but something else, too. I realized that God had allowed everything to happen to bring me to this point. I had everything I thought meant so much; now what would I do?"

He paused before continuing, "There are still so many who need shelter, and though food isn't nearly the problem it once was, housing is. I could build a huge house and have families come and live there, but I realized it wasn't what I wanted. I want to divide the money between some families who need it."

Alaina's mouth parted. "Are you serious?"

Jack's throat thickened. "I mean it so much it hurts. I've learned my lesson, Alaina. I want to help someone else. I'll still keep a portion for us, but the rest will go to help those in need. To rebuild life for those so shaken by the disaster."

Tears shimmered in her eyes, and Jack felt the rightness of his words in every part of his body. "We'll move away, you, me, and your mother. Frank and Missy and Sam, too, if they want to come. Then we can settle down and make a home."

Alaina brushed her hand across her cheeks. "Where will we go?"

He shrugged. "Wherever you want to go. We'll travel until we find a place. God will show us."

She hugged herself and stared out over Johnstown, and when she finally met his gaze, Jack saw the spark of a smile. "Aren't you forgetting something?"

He chuckled. "I was wondering if you would notice." He closed the distance between them and grasped her by the waist. "I think this is going on the third time I'm going to ask, so I'm hoping for a better answer."

She reached as if to smack his shoulder, but he captured her hand and raised it to his lips. As he stared into her dark eyes, he glimpsed a future of peace and commitment, not only to her but also to God and to his fellow man. "Alaina?"

"I would be most honored to become your wife."

epilogue

Dear Aunt Jo,

We hope this letter finds you doing well. We've settled
down in Kansas for a space of time. Sam and Missy love the
prairie grasses and fresh country air, and Frank has them
going to the schoolhouse down the road, something they both
seem to enjoy very much. I think Frank is pleased with the
idea of staying on here. Jack thinks it would be a good place
to put down some roots and start a family. I can honestly say
that my heart has already learned to love the prairie, and
staying here would be a joy.

Mother is doing quite well. In the two weeks since we
arrived, she has taken more to sewing, even completing a
new dress for Missy. She still doesn't say much, but I suspect
time will heal that as well. Time and Frank. Yes, you read
that right. I think the two of them are finding that their
hearts aren't quite so lonely when they're together. It's a
wonder to behold, Auntie. Momma's face takes on such a
beautiful gentleness when Frank is near.

Jack just lit the lantern for me to write by, but I think
he really wants to go for a short walk. By the way, he and
Frank have been whispering lately. My guess is they've found
some land on which to build. But I wouldn't want to spoil
Jack's surprise and will write no more until I know for sure.

As you will see, I've included a likeness of us. We posed for
it the day after Jack and I were married, at the insistence
of the man taking pictures of Johnstown. He said everyone
should have a memory of their special day. It was a special
day, Auntie. In the midst of Johnstown's rise to its former
glory, we stood on Green Hill and were joined as husband
and wife. Many of the townspeople were there to share our

happiness and, we hope, glean a bit of joy to give their hearts a new promise for all their tomorrows.

It's been a long road for all of us, but we're praying for strength and grace, and for Momma's complete healing, though if Frank has anything to do with it, that prayer is being answered as I write.

We send our love.
Alaina Kelly

A Letter To Our Readers

Dear Reader:

In order that we might better contribute to your reading enjoyment, we would appreciate your taking a few minutes to respond to the following questions. We welcome your comments and read each form and letter we receive. When completed, please return to the following:

Fiction Editor
Heartsong Presents
PO Box 719
Uhrichsville, Ohio 44683

1. Did you enjoy reading *Promise of Tomorrow* by S. Dionne Moore?
   ❏ Very much! I would like to see more books by this author!
   ❏ Moderately. I would have enjoyed it more if

   _____

   _____

   _____

2. Are you a member of **Heartsong Presents**? ❏ Yes ❏ No
   If no, where did you purchase this book? _____

   _____

3. How would you rate, on a scale from 1 (poor) to 5 (superior), the cover design? _____

4. On a scale from 1 (poor) to 10 (superior), please rate the following elements.

   ____ Heroine   ____ Plot
   ____ Hero   ____ Inspirational theme
   ____ Setting   ____ Secondary characters

5. These characters were special because? _____

_____

_____

6. How has this book inspired your life? _____

_____

_____

7. What settings would you like to see covered in future
   Heartsong Presents books? _____

_____

_____

8. What are some inspirational themes you would like to see
   treated in future books? _____

_____

_____

9. Would you be interested in reading other **Heartsong
   Presents** titles? ❑ Yes ❑ No

10. Please check your age range:
    ❑ Under 18   ❑ 18-24
    ❑ 25-34   ❑ 35-45
    ❑ 46-55   ❑ Over 55

Name _____

Occupation _____

Address _____

City, State, Zip _____

E-mail _____

SILVER MOUNTAINS

3 stories in 1

There are three siblings bicker over their father's inheritance. Can God show these siblings where true treasures lies?

Historical, paperback, 352 pages, 5³⁄₁₆" x 8"